COPYRIGHTS ©
2016 by Tommy Shorter
All rights reserved
No parts of this book may be used or reproduced without permission except in the case of quotes in articles or reviews. For more information, Tommy Shorter PO BOX 17174 Pittsburgh, Pennsylvania, 15235

Cover Design: Ashley Taylor

ACKNOWLEDGEMENTS

First and foremost, I want to thank God for providing me with the knowledge, wisdom and the will to make this dream of mine come true. There was a time when I thought this wouldn't happen, but it shows that when you work hard, the results will come.

I also want to thank the federal government for giving me so much time to think. Who knows what I would've become, if in fact I'd still be alive. Now I'm at peace within, ready to share my visions with the world.

Thanks to my family for being supportive throughout my life, but mainly during my decade of being incarcerated. The financial aid, correspondence and everything else you have provided me with has given me the privilege of remaining sane, which afforded me with the opportunity to write and complete this book.

To my friends and loved one's who have been supportive to some degree, I thank you dearly. Just the constant encouragement that brighter days are near gave me that drive. We did it!

To my three children Angela, Tommy, and Tommi Nicole; it means the world to me that during my absence, I always felt present. I love y'all and I sincerely appreciate y'all giving me the will to keep fighting, even though I wanted to quit a long time ago. Chase your dreams, because they do come true. Thanks for giving me beautiful grandchildren as well.

I want to give an extra special thanks to my main man Ray-Ray Sweetenburg for helping me make this book a reality. Without you taking time to type it for me and assuring me that I had quality material, I'd be still at square one. I've been a lot of places, seen a whole lot, but never have I met a good dude the caliber of you. We're a team for life my dude, much respect.

For those that continue to pray for my downfall, just know that you'll never be able to get time and energy back. Every moment we have on earth is vital (of utmost importance), so be mindful of how you embrace your journey; you might not like that destination. On top of that, I'm determined to win.

To my beautiful sister Ashley, I thank you dearly for the time and effort that you put into the book and I can never thank you enough, but I can express my unlimited love and appreciation that I have for you. I don't know what I would've done without you. It is an honor to have you as my sister and business partner. Your sacrifice will pay off in the long run and keep me grounded as well. One down and nine more to go sis!

DEDICATION

NEVER FORGOTTEN

This is dedicated to my family and friends that are no longer with me here on earth. I'm talking about Ron, Beam, Mike, Manny, Truck, Wop and Jug, I pray y'all know what our relationship is worth. Cousins Ty and Eric Swan, Mark and Pook Ross, Pretty Rob, Tyke and all the rest of y'all who have impacted my life. I assure everyone that y'all souls may rest in peace, because you'll forever, I mean forever, live through Ice.

Grandma, Daddy T, Eric, my two beautiful aunts, Cousin Niecy and Diondra, I love y'all dearly too.

Dealing with deaths and all my hardships have made me the man I am, and memories of y'all have helped me get through

It's been 12 ½ years of five percent joy, ten percent anger, twenty-five percent bitterness, and sixty percent will to survive and succeed.

I still remember the day my daughter's mom shared some encouraging words, when she told me that a little faith is all hope needs.

But as I continue on my journey and still evolve as a man, a writer, a father, etc..., y'all will be with me every step of the way.

And even though y'all are not physically along for the ride, just know that I'll continue to love and appreciate y'all tomorrow, as much as I do today

Every single day it's an emotional struggle to stay sane, to not do dead time, and to not sit in my jail cell rotting.

All the pleasant and fond memories of us carries me through, but no matter what transitions I go through in life, y'all are.

Never Forgotten

(Internal and Spiritual Love)

PROLOGUE

JUNE 10, 1981…

"Here baby, open your mouth. You have to eat so you can feel better," Karen spoke, as she fed her daughter Keya the remainder of chicken soup.

They were suddenly startled when the front door slammed; but knowing it had to be Keya's father entering the house.

"Mommy, that's daddy," Keya shouted in a cheerful voice after the startling affect went away.

"I know baby. Just lie down and rest for a while. I'll be back to check on you in a minute."

"Okay mommy."

Keya jumped under the covers and smiled as her mother planted a warm kiss on her cheek. As Karen left the room, she left the door open slightly, in route to go greet Kenny.

"Where the fuck is my food at?" Kenny asked, highly upset.

"It's cooking right now baby. Keya's sick, so I had to take care of her," Karen explained.

"You could've been had that done! You don't do shit but sit around and talk on the phone all day!" He snapped.

"I said your food will be ready in a few minutes!" Karen responded in a smart tone.

"I'm not in the mood for your bullshit! I just lost three hundred dollars shooting dice and I'm hungry!"

"Don't blame me because you lost your money! Your stomach can hold off for a few extra minutes!"

"Just shut the fuck up!" Kenny barked.

"You need to go back outside and take that bad attitude out on whoever won your money!"

"Hi daddy," Keya shouted as she came running towards him with a huge smile from ear to ear.

"Keya, go to your room and play while I talk to your mother."

"Daddy, I want to show you something that I made for you."

"I said go to your room! Now!" He screamed.

"You don't have to talk to her like that! She's only six years old!"

"Shut the fuck up! I run this house! You need to worry about getting my food together!"

"Yeah whatever."

Kenny didn't like her response, so he cocked his hand back and slapped the shit out of Karen. As she tried to defend herself, the slaps turned into punches that connected with her jaw, lips and head. When she fell to the floor he started kicking her in the ribs and legs.

"Now get up and get my food on the table! He screamed.

Keya never saw her father act like that before and all the screaming and hollering frightened her. She jumped on her bed and hid under the covers, crying uncontrollably.

Karen quickly cleaned herself up and prepared his food. After being assured that he was satisfied, she trotted towards the bedroom to check on Keya.

"Come here baby. Mommy's here."

Keya jumped in her mother's arms, as tears were streaming down her cheeks.

"Daddy didn't mean it baby. He's sorry."

Karen hummed a few songs until Keya went to sleep, then tucked her in bed. After that she cleaned up the house, followed by a nice hot bath. The bruises on her face were barely noticeable, but she was aching badly. As she soaked in her bubble bath, she cried softly. Kenny came in and grabbed the wash cloth and began to bathe her.

"Baby, I'm sorry. I didn't mean to put my hands on you."

Karen didn't respond, she just kept her eyes closed tight.

"I was pissed about the money I lost and I blacked out when you kept talking back to me. Whatever I have to do to make it up to you I will. Please just tell me that you forgive me baby. It's eating me up inside."

Karen stayed silent, so he continued to wash her up, then helped her dry off when he was finish. When they got to their bedroom he planted soft kisses on her neck and face. She eventually gave in and started kissing him back. He gently laid her on the bed and began making love to her. Each one of his strokes were slow and affectionate.

"Do it feel good baby?"

"Yes, she whispered softly.

It felt so good that she held him tight and started crying.

"Kenny promise me that you'll never put your hands on me again?" Karen asked, through lustful sobs.

"I promise baby. I'll never allow myself to get that angry to where I would want to put my hands on your again."

Kenny stayed true to his word and never hit Karen again. He even went the extra mile spoiling

Karen and Keya as much as he could. He used that as leverage to stay out late at night and there were times when he didn't even come home at all. Karen's friends constantly told her that he was cheating, but when she confronted him, Kenny would quickly deny it.

The truth eventually surfaced when he got into a fight over one of the girls he was messing with. The fight cost him dearly too. He stabbed the guy eight times in the stomach and chest area, which got him sentenced to 3½ to 7 years in state prison.

Karen went to visit him faithfully for the first few months, but she fell off after getting involved in another relationship. Kenny constantly wrote letters and poured his heart out to her, but it didn't do him any good. He had kept her secluded for six long years while he ran the streets and cheated, but now at the age of twenty-four, she was ready to get out and enjoy herself. He was able to see Keya when his mother visited, but Karen was officially done with him.

Her new life wasn't as smooth as a transition that she thought it would be. Karen hooked up with a petty street hustler named Eddie, a real slick talker who eventually turned her out on weed, heroin and alcohol. He beat on her from time to time, until she decided their relationship had ran its course. Her decision became final when Eddie threw her down a flight of stairs while she was three months pregnant. Fortunately, the baby was okay. Karen managed to get rid of Eddie, but she was unable to shake her drug habit. After she had Eddie Jr., Karen was in and out of different relationships until Kenny finally came home. They got back together and Karen gave birth to another handsome baby boy. Nevertheless, Kenny quickly grew tired of her and left them all alone.

Karen started drinking heavily; she constantly entertained different men and always verbally and sometimes physically abused Keya and her two younger brothers. Although Keya was only eleven years old, Karen would try to force her daughter to have sex with different men. Whenever she was told to do so, Keya would jump out the window and run away. Most of the time Keya ran to Kenny's mother's house where she would stay for weeks at a time before she returned home. Karen always welcomed her daughter back with open arms, even though she'd be so angry that she could kill Keya. Whenever Keya's grandmother would leave, Karen beat the hell out of her.

"Don't you ever embarrass me like that again girl! The next time I'll kill you! Do you hear me?" Karen barked.

"Yes, I hear you mom! Please don't hit me no more!" Keya pleaded.

"Do what I tell you and I won't have to!"

In the weeks to come, Keya wasn't allowed off the front steps. She had to clean up the house and take out the garbage on a regular basis. Her mother kept a tight leash on her especially when Keya really started to develop physically. Karen's male friends constantly made advances at Keya and when she confided in her mother about it, Karen would accuse her of lying and utter disparaging names at her.

One night Karen and one of her many friends staggered into Keya's room. She ordered Keya to get undressed and threatened to kill her if she refused.

"Mom, why are you making me do this?" Keya cried out.

"Just shut the hell up and do what I told you!" Karen ordered her.

Keya wanted to jump out the window and run to her grandmother's house like she normally did, but Karen was blocking that exit. With no other alternative left, she ran to a corner in her room and cried her eyes out. Her mother grabbed her by her long, silky black hair and practically slapped the taste out her mouth.

"Get over there and do what I told you to do! Now!"

Keya repeatedly begged the man not to do it, but his patience had started to wear thin.

"I don't have all day Karen, make her get those clothes off!"

"Please don't do this to me! Please!" Keya begged.

He then pushed her hard on the bed, pulled down her panties, then forced himself inside her. Keya wanted to scream when he first entered her, but she laid there and fought through the pain. He had a terrible body odor and she couldn't wait for him to finish so she could go soak in the bath tub. He smelled like stale cigarettes and vomit. After he released inside of her, he put his clothes on and handed Karen two hundred dollars.

"Thanks Frank. I'll see you a little later," Karen spoke with a drunken slur in her voice.

"Hey Karen. What would it cost for both of y'all together?" Frank asked before leaving.

"You know you can't handle this pussy. How do you think you'll be able to handle both of us together?"

"I want both of y'all together."

"We'll talk about that later Frank. Right now is not a good time."

Karen walked Frank to the door and showed him out, then came back to Keya's room.

"Come here baby. Everything's going to be okay. You're just becoming a woman quicker than others your age. It had to be this way Keya, because without a real job it's hard around here. This is the only way to put food on the table. We have to use what we got, to get what we want. Your dad ain't worth shit! That no good son of a bitch don't give us a dime! You'll see when you get older that men don't give a fuck about you! They become very possessive and beat on women like it's a normal thing to do! It all started with your father beating on me, and then the beatings trickled down to all my relationships. Keya, I am thirty one years old and I've been through more shit than my grandmother has. Baby I'm going to show you how to survive in this world and not be controlled by all the egotistical men that prey on women. You might hate me right now, but you'll understand in the long run. Now go get yourself cleaned up."

Before Keya got up to go run her bath water, she had to wait until her legs stopped shaking uncontrollably. On top of that, her vagina was throbbing. After waiting for about five minutes she managed to get up and go to the bathroom. When she first jumped into the hot water it stung for a few seconds until it finally started to soothe her. Keya shook from anger, pain and confusion as tears rapidly rolled down her cheeks. She couldn't understand why her mother would make her do something like that. She just sat and watched while the stranger took her innocence.

After cleaning the bath tub Keya managed to go back to her room without running into her mother.

She went into her bedroom and locked the door behind her. Keya could still smell Frank's awful scent in the room, so she went to the window and cracked it open. The cold winter air brought a breath of fresh air into the small area. As she glanced at the bed where she had just been violated, Keya flipped it over and found a comfortable spot in the corner of her room where she finally fell asleep.

Over the next couple days she found the nerve to confide in her best friend Robin. When she got off the phone with Keya, Robin shared the horrible information with her mother.

"She doesn't need to be in that house," Robin's mother expressed. "Robin get her back on the phone for me."

When Robin called back, Keya answered on the first ring.

"Keya, my mom wants to talk to you," Robin told her.

"Hello Keya. This is Momma Sue baby. Get all your clothes packed. You're coming with us."

"O-Okay. Ms. Sue, can you please hurry? That man is at my house again."

"I'm on my way baby. It shouldn't take me no more than five minutes. Just keep your door locked until I get there."

"Okay."

As soon as Keya got off the phone with Robin's mother, she locked her bedroom door and began to pack her clothes. A few minutes later she heard the footsteps of her mother and Frank approaching her room.

"Open the door Keya!" Her mother shouted, after realizing that Keya's bedroom door was locked. "Don't make me knock this mother fucker down!" She rambled on with threats.

Keya ignored her mother's promising words and continued to pack her belongings. While dumping her clothes in bags, she silently prayed that Ms. Sue would hurry up and come get her.

"You better open this door right now before I come in there and kick your ass!" Her mother screamed.

Keya contemplated jumping out the window and running like she normally did, but instead she just continued to throw her clothes in bags.

"Kick it down Frank!" Keya heard her mother demand.

After about twenty attempts the cheap door finally gave in, Keya hurried and hid the bags she packed then sat on her bed, scared for her life. As they made their way into her room, Keya could see the rage in her mother's eyes.

"Please don't make me do this again mom! Please!"

"Shut up!" Karen yelled at the top of her lungs.

"I won't hurt you," Frank said, as he sat down beside Keya.

She smelt that familiar odor of Frank, which literally made her sick to her stomach. She eased away from him a little, trying not to make eye contact with her mother. Frank started easing towards Keya, but he took his attention off her when he heard someone knocking loudly on the door.

"They'll leave," Karen said dryly. "I'm not expecting more company."

Keya used the brief distraction to her advantage. She grabbed the thick, empty Pepsi bottle that she drunk the night before and hit Frank across the head as hard as she could. Karen stood there in shock as the blood ran down Frank's face. She didn't even realize that Keya ran pass her to go open the front door. Ms. Sue rushed into the house, along with two police officers. Keya ran into Ms. Sue's open arms and cried with joy.

"My mom let that man do bad things to me," Keya chanted repeatedly.

"What the hell is going on here!" Karen yelled as she entered the room.

"How could you be so evil?" Ms. Sue asked. "She's just a baby and she's your daughter!"

"You need to mind your fuckin' business and get the hell out of my house! Get over here Keya!" Karen shouted in an authoritative voice, which sharpened Keya's fear.

The officers had heard enough, plus the alcohol on Karen's breath was strong. One of the officers stayed in the living room and kept a close eye on Karen, while the other one searched the small apartment.

"You need to be getting that bitch out my house!" Karen spat.

The officer just stood between them and ignored Karen. Ms. Sue ignored her as well, focusing all of her attention on comforting Keya.

"I got him!" The officer shouted.

He caught Frank running into the bathroom attempting to climb out the bathroom window. When it was all said and done, Frank and Karen were taken into custody and charged with sexual assault of a minor. In the beginning Karen tried to deny everything, but after hours of interrogation about Keya's bedroom door being shattered into pieces and Frank's injury she finally confessed to everything.

With the permission of her grandmother, Keya moved in with Ms. Sue and her daughter Robin, while her two brothers Eddie and Kenny moved in with their Uncle Greg, who recently moved back to Pittsburgh from New York. He wanted his niece to move in with him too, but they all decided it was best that she stay in an environment where there were females present. Being that Robin was her best friend, it was a perfect situation.

The Evolution of Keya Gibson
Chapter 1

August 23, 1989

I was an emotional wreck for quite a while after the terrible ordeal that I went through with my mother and Frank. It was something that a normal thirteen-year-old didn't go through. When Ms. Sue eventually came and rescued me from that sick and degrading experience, I could feel life would get better for me from that moment on. My fourteenth birthday was the best of all birthdays, thanks mostly to my new family. For one; the atmosphere was a much better one by far. Although my mom was hopefully rotting away in jail, a part of her still lived within me. Because of her I had a huge grudge against all boys and men, but Ms. Sue did a great job of protecting me from my greatest fears. As my body went through its stages of development, my grudges and fears became cravings.

My family, meaning my Uncle Greg and Ms. Sue took good care of me. Financially I wanted for nothing and when my freshman year of high school came around before my fifteenth birthday I became a fashion icon, or so I thought. My Uncle did our school shopping in New York, so I had things long before they hit the stores in Pittsburgh. Most of the females looked at me with envy whenever I sported different flavors of Jordache, Levi's, Sassoon and Gloria Vanderbilt jeans just to name a few. I couldn't help it that God produced this beautiful light brown-skinned, five-foot-two-inch, one hundred and twelve-pound princess to model those clothing lines. That's not even counting the leather skirts, pants, cute shirts and sweaters I wore. I also had a variety of Lotto's, Fila's and Diadora's. My only fashion competition was Robin and my other friend Janet, who also got their clothes from New York.

Robin was about three inches taller than me, with long legs and great calves. She also had the perfect breast and pretty white teeth. Robin didn't have a big ole ghetto booty, but it sat nice on her one hundred twenty-two-pound frame.

Janet was also light brown-skinned like me and Robin, but she was the thickest out of the three of us. She was around five feet four inches tall and weighed one hundred thirty-three pounds. When I say that Janet's thick in the thighs that's an understatement.

One day we came to school and really had heads turning when we strolled through with our sheepskin coats on and our big bamboo earrings with our names in them. I loved it because all of the movement stopped whenever we came through. There was never a time that I didn't come to school looking fine as ever. Being that my ass and hips were my biggest assets, boys couldn't help but gaze at my tight-fitting Levi's and my shirt that was tied in a knot, which exposed just a little bit of my flat toned stomach. As me and Robin entered the cafeteria, I was approached by the star quarterback of our varsity football team. His name was Mike and he was the most popular guy in the school. He was also one of the best players on the basketball team. He had a great physique and he also dressed fly, which was a super plus. Mike was only a junior and the teachers gave him as much praise as the students did. Nevertheless, none of them tolerated him being late for classes and he was required to push harder than everyone else, being that he had so much influence on practically the entire school. He made his way towards me while Robin and I stood in the lunch line to get our food.

"Let me help you carry your tray?" Mike offered.

"No thank you."

"Please," he pleaded.

"Okay," I said nervously and telling myself that I gave in too quickly.

"Do you mind sitting with me at my table?" He added.

"I .... I-."

"Go ahead Key, I'll be at our table with Janet. I need a few laughs," Robin told me.

"Thanks Robin. I'll take good care of her," Mike swore.

"How do you know my name?" Robin asked.

"I find out everything about people that I feel I need to know. Y'all freshmen are real popular around here."

"Whatever, Mr. know everybody. You just worry about treating my sister right. Me and my other sister will be watching from our table too."

"Keya are you ready? Our food is getting cold," Mike said, looking away from Robin.

"Yeah I'm ready. I'll see you later sis."

Mike walked me over to a table where a couple of his friends were sitting at. As we began to sit down, they finished up their food and gave us the table to ourselves.

"You must be a very important woman."

"Why do you say that?" I asked out of curiosity.

"Look what I had to go through just to be alone with you for a few minutes."

"My sisters are very protective of me."

"I see. Robin's been watching us since we sat down. Look at her."

"I do the same thing for her," I told him, as I took a bite out of my turkey sandwich.

"Do you have a boyfriend or somebody you be talking to?"

"Maybe, maybe not."

"Which one is it?"

"Which one do you want it to be?"

"Close your eyes for a second, you have something on your eyelash," he told me.

As I closed my eyes so he could remove whatever was there, I felt his lips press softly against mines. It felt a little awkward at first, but as he continued to give me light pecks on my lips, I started kissing him back. It was my first time ever kissing, so when our tongues met I just followed his motion. Our tongues and mouths danced to a rhythm. I swear it was like poetry in motion. I felt at ease, relaxed, like I didn't have a worry in the world. As our mouths separated, I kept my eyes closed to savor the moment. Mike gently ran his hand through my hair as he spoke.

"Does that answer your question?"

"Yes," I whispered, finally opening my eyes.

"I don't want you to give me an answer right now about if you mess with somebody. I can wait until I pick you up after school, if that's cool with you?"

"It sounds good to me."

"Okay, I'll see you later then."

As I got up to walk away, he grabbed my tray out my hand and sat it on the table. Afterwards he gently placed his hands on my shoulders and pulled me close to him. Once again, he placed his soft, moist lips onto mines. The kiss wasn't as affectionate as the first one, but it was still good. As our lip locking came to an end, I made my way over to Janet and Robin.

"Well, well. I see our mouths don't just open to talk and eat with."

"Shut up Janet! Don't start your stuff," I told her.

"That's so sweet. Your first kiss is with the most popular guy in school," Robin joined in.

"Tell us about it," Janet insisted. "Is he a good kisser? Is his lips soft? And most importantly, did he have fresh breath?"

"To the first question, it's yes. The second one is none of your business and his breath didn't stink. As a matter of fact, everything was perfect, He told me to close my eyes because I had something on my eyelash, and then he kissed me. He kept kissing me, so I started kissing him back. We're meeting up again after school today."

"Mike is smooth. He hit you with the playa, playa move," Janet teased.

"We can finish talking about this a little later, Lunch is almost over," Robin alarmed us.

Janet got her last words in, then we all scampered off in different directions to our classes. For me, it seemed like every second that went by took an hour to go by. I was totally in another world, because all I could think about was Mike and his soft lips. "Damn, I loved his lips." As I sat there in a daze, I mentally prayed that my English and Social Studies classes would hurry up and end, because I had Phys. Ed. last period.

All three classes eventually came and went. Me, Janet and Robin met up in the hallway before we went outside to go meet Mike. The school grounds were almost cleared out and there was still no sign of Mike. I didn't let Janet and Robin know it, but I was overwhelmed with disappointment. I kept beating myself up about being played for a fool. It was too good to be true for the most popular guy in school to want me; a ninth grader at that. The show he put on in the cafeteria was probably to show that he could have whoever he wanted. As the crowd began to get thinner, we headed towards the school bus that awaited us. I accepted the fact that I got played and even the look on both of my sisters faces showed some concern for me. When we finally reached the bottom of the steps, my heart nearly jumped out my chest. Mike and his boys were in a royal blue Chevy

Blazer with the roof off trying to flag us down. We ran over and jumped in the truck. The front seat was reserved just for me.

"I thought I missed you. Did you think I wasn't going to show up?"

"Yeah, I thought you played me."

"You'll never have to guess with me. If I say something, I try to stick to my word. It has to be a real emergency to have me go against my word. Plus, if I wouldn't have showed up I couldn't get my answer."

"I might freeze to death before I get to tell you."

"Sorry about that. We got the truck washed inside and out, but the roof wasn't done yet. If we would've stayed and waited I would've missed you. If that would've happened, I wouldn't be able to sleep at night," Mike mentioned before pinching my cheek.

"Yeah right, you think you got game huh?"

"Nah, I'm dead serious. After them kisses, I couldn't stop thinking about you."

"I couldn't stop thinking about you either," I revealed, not knowing if that was a good idea.

"So, does that mean you don't have a boyfriend or somebody you talk to?"

"Well actually, I have a few boyfriends."

"Damn, you doing it like that? You get around huh?"

"I'm just playing. I don't have a boyfriend or somebody I talk to, and no I don't get around. I never had a boyfriend before."

"Do you want one?"

"It depends on who he is," I teased. "Do you have a girlfriend or people you talk to? Please don't lie to me either."

"I had a girlfriend, but we broke up a few weeks ago."

"Why?"

"Because she came too easy. It's cool to be attracted to someone who's popular, but I don't want a girlfriend who does any and everything I tell her to do. Everyone has to be able to make their own decisions most of the time. One of the things that I like about you is that what I do don't impress you all like that."

"How do you know?" I asked skeptically.

"Because when I first tried to make eye contact with you, it was like you didn't even notice me."

I remained quiet as we pulled in the car wash to get the roof put back on. We all got out the truck and sat in the small waiting area.

"You still never answered my question," he whispered softly in my ear.

"I want you," I found myself saying. The words just slipped out my mouth, I couldn't help myself.

Mike smiled, then gave me a few pecks on my lips. As we continued to converse while waiting for the truck to get done, I noticed Janet and Robin exchanging phone numbers with Mike's two friends.

Ty, who exchanged numbers with Janet, was the star wide receiver and one of the four captains on the football team. He was six feet two inches tall, with a nice athletic build.

Mont, who Robin was kicking it with was much shorter, but more compact, standing at five feet nine inches tall. He was the star running back and was also a captain on the team.

Mike was the tallest of the three. He was barely two inches taller than Ty and of course he was one of the captains. The kicker was the fourth captain, mainly because he was a senior who had been on the team all four years.

When the roof was done, they took us to McDonald's, and then dropped us off. Janet wasn't sure if her mother was home from work yet, so we all got out around the corner from her house. Janet stayed on Dickson Street and we lived on Woodland Avenue. Momma Sue was very protective of us and getting dropped off by our house was out of the question. We gave them some goodbye kisses, then walked home.

After me and Robin finished up our homework and chores, we walked two and a half blocks until we made it to Janet's house. When we got there she was on the phone with Ty. She was smiling from ear to ear too.

"You in love already girl and it's only been like three hours!" Robin shouted out, putting her on the spot.

"Ty, I'll call you back! Robin won't get out my conversation!"

"Don't be lying to him!" Robin blurted out.

"Here, somebody wants to talk to you," Janet relayed to Robin.

"Hello," Robin spoke, knowing exactly who it was.

"Did you forget about me already?"

"Hey Mont, no," Robin blushed. "I was going to call you when I got back home."

"I called you twice already baby. If this is how things are going to be, I rather we just be friends."

"Come see me right now and we can talk in person until I call you tonight."

"Alright, tell your girls that I'm bringing Mike and Ty with me."

"We'll be waiting," Robin assured him, still smiling.

It wasn't long before we met them at the same spot that they dropped us off at earlier in the day. They drove us around before we went to Allegheny Center Mall. Once we got to the mall we stopped in Dream Machine to play a few arcade games. There weren't many people there, so we were pretty much able to play whatever games we wanted to play. The fellas took turns competing on the basketball game while we cheered them on in the background. We finished up our day at Dream Machine on the driving game. By them taking time to show us how to drive, it was a perfect opportunity for them to get their grind on. Although we were well aware of what was going on, I have to admit that I loved having Mike pressed up against me. I guess the horrible experience that I had with my mother and Frank only made me hornier for someone I could really develop feelings for. It had only been a few hours since I even met Mike, but I could feel that he was what was missing in my life.

It was starting to get late and we were getting closer to our 8:30 curfew. Mike and his boys had a little more breathing room, but Momma Sue and Janet's mom Aunt Jackie didn't play no games. Mont, who was driving, parked the truck around the corner from Janet's house again, then we all engaged in a fifteen-minute kissing session. Man I loved kissing

Mike and it had only been our first day at it. During our session, he taught me how to slowly glide my tongue across his. The best part was when he grabbed my ass with his strong hands and pulled me close to him.

When the festivities finally ended, we walked Janet home, then made it home ourselves in record time. We ate the smothered pork chops with gravy, mashed potatoes and stuffing that Momma Sue cooked. After we ate, we took our baths then jumped on the phone. We both had our own phones in our rooms, so we didn't have to take turns. I talked to Mike until 1:00am, at least that was the last time I looked at the clock.

When Robin woke me up the following morning for school, my phone was off the hook.

"I see you had a long night on the phone too," Robin said, standing over me with a devilish grin on her face.

"Yeah, I stayed on the phone until at least one in the morning."

"Me and Mont talked until a little after twelve, then my eyes started getting heavy," Robin elaborated.

"My eyes kept getting heavy too, but I stayed on the phone anyway," I explained before getting out of bed.

"Keya, I think I'm in love."

"Yeah right, it ain't even been twenty-four hours yet."

"You're right, but I like him a whole lot," Robin said excitedly.

"I like Mike too."

"Did he mention anything to you about the party?"

"What party?" I asked in amazement.

"The party over Ty's cousin's house."

"I must've fell asleep on that part."

"Well Keya, you need to hurry up and get dressed so we can eat some hot food and talk to mom together about staying out a little later so we can go to the party."

"Okay. I'll meet you downstairs in fifteen minutes."

I hurried and got myself together, which really didn't take me long because I took my bath the night before. When I made my way downstairs, mom was preparing our food. She fixed us some french toast, cheese eggs, bacon and cream of wheat. Robin had milk with her breakfast, but I was too busy gobbling my food down to drink anything. I was eating like it was my last meal. When I noticed how Momma Sue was staring at us, I immediately stopped eating.

"Who's the boys?" She asked, as if she knew everything that was going on.

"Huh, what boys?" We both managed to say simultaneously.

"I know those looks from anywhere. I'm a female too, remember. Let's hear it. Tell me about these boys."

"My friend's name is Mont," Robin started rambling. "He's the star running back on the varsity football team at our school."

"Mines is the star quarterback on the same team and his name is Mike. He's pretty cool. I like him."

"You don't have to tell me. I know that couldn't have been Janet on the phone all night."

"How did you know?" I asked.

"Mom knows everything, it's my job," she said with a confident smile. "I was waiting for y'all to act like y'all didn't want to get up for school this morning."

"We know how important our education is."

"What do you want Robin?"

"If we let you meet them can we stay out a little later and go to the party with them tonight?"

"Bring them by after school and we'll see. I might let Damon have a chat with them."

"Thanks mom," we both said while giving her a hug.

We gathered up all the things that we needed to take with us, then headed out the door for school. I kept telling myself that today was going to be a great day.

Mr. Damon was Momma Sue's boyfriend, but he didn't live with us. Me and Robin still felt connected to him because he always took time out to take us to the movies and pretty much got us anything we wanted. Because of the horrible ordeal that I experienced as a child, Mr. Damon made it his top priority to make me feel as comfortable as possible. It was also one of the reasons he didn't live with us. I always felt the need to assure him that I was okay and that I loved him like a father. Robin felt the same way as I did, because like mines, her father Earl was never a part of her life. Those were scars that had healed a long time ago for us. Mr. Damon was all the father me and Robin needed. In fact, during our Saturday night at the movies with Momma Sue's permission, we had plans to ask him to move in with us.

That morning when we went to school I felt exhausted, but when we strolled through the spacious hallways I was full of life. We still had a fifteen-minute grace period before our first class started, so we hung out in our regular spot where everybody would notice us. A few guys made it their business to stop in front of us to share their weak pickup lines, but they got the message real quick when I rolled my eyes and sucked my teeth. I was loud enough for Momma Sue to hear me from at home. As the fifteen minutes began to wind down I started to feel drained again. My first class made it even worse when Mr. Parker talked the entire time. He probably would've lectured us for another two or three hours if the bell for class to end didn't ring. I was so thankful that class was over, because my treat came when I saw Mike walking towards me. He looked drained too, but his expression turned into a bright smile when we finally made eye contact.

"Hey baby, where have you been all my life?" He asked.

"Who me?" I asked, pretending to be looking for the person he was talking to.

"Yeah you cutey," he said while reaching over to pinch me on my cheeks as usual. It was something I was growing fond of.

"Do you always ask girls that?"

"Only the ones I like."

I rolled my eyes at him and started walking towards my next class. As he yelled out my name, I began to walk faster. He caught up with me and turned me around so I could face him.

"I was just playing," he told me with the cutest sad face.

"Well you shouldn't play with me like that."

"Okay, it won't happen again."

"It better not. Hey, why didn't you tell me about the party?"

"I tried to, but you were too busy snoring in my ear."

"No I wasn't," I said, giving him a gentle push.

"Yes you were. I can still hear your snoring in my ear."

"Whatever Mike. Are you busy after school?"

"Nope, why what's up?"

"My mother wants to meet you to see if she feels comfortable letting us stay out a little later tonight."

"Wow, I get to meet your mom? What should I expect? Is she mean?"

"She's a nice person. She's only mean when we're doing stuff we're not supposed to be doing," I replied honestly.

"I'll be ready when school is out."

"Okay."

He walked me to my class and gave me one of them special kisses that constantly drove me crazy.

The rest of the day sped by for me. At lunch we spent our break practicing the cheerleading steps we came up with. Through the crowd of people that surrounded us we saw Mike and his boys watching, so we got a little extra with our moves. When we did this one particular routine where we winded our hips like a reggae dancer everybody's eyes were glued on us. We realized that we had to stop, because the crowd around us was getting too thick. As we made our way through the crowd everyone congratulated us. Mike was waiting patiently for me with a huge smile on his face. He took his varsity jacket off and threw it around my shoulders.

"Giving you my jacket officially makes you my girl."

"Thank you."

"Come on, let me walk you to class."

As we got near my class, I noticed that he was licking his lips. I decided to tease him a little bit just to see how he would react.

"I'm saving all my kisses until school is out," I told him as he prepared to kiss me.

"What! You have to give me a kiss, you're my girl now."

"I know, but I want you to wait until we get out of school."

He pulled me close to him and held me real tight. It felt so good that I didn't want him to let go. Plus, he smelled so good.

"I'll take that hug for now baby," he said before giving me a pinch on my cheeks.

"Can't wait to see you later."

As I started walking away he gave me a nice tap on my butt. To assure him that I liked it, I turned around to reveal the seductive smile on my face. He winked at me, then displayed his heart-breaking smile, then walked away.

The rest of my day continued to fly by, which delighted me, because I couldn't wait to lock lips with my boyfriend. During my last period class, this one particular girl just kept staring at me. She made me feel uncomfortable, so I decided to approach her.

"Is there a reason why you keep staring at me?" I ask with some hostility in my tone.

"Because they're my eyes," she answered back with an attitude of her own.

"You better work on fixing them," I warned her.

"And if I don't?"

I didn't like the response she gave me, so I cocked back and hit her as hard as I could. From that point on I blacked out. I grabbed a handful of her hair and continued punching her in the face. All I could envision was my mom and Frank, which made every punch more intense. When it was all said and done, the only thing that I remembered was the principal calling home to tell Momma Sue that I was suspended for fighting. I could hear her hollering through the phone asking him to repeat himself. I could only imagine what her facial expression looked like when he repeated to her that I was in a fight.

After he hung up, the principal gave me another lecture and reminded me that I was suspended for three days, then I was permitted to leave. Janet and Robin were waiting for me outside the office and looked like they were ready to do some fighting of their own.

"Come on, let's go beat them hoes down!" Janet snapped.

"It was four of them huddled up outside, so let's go see what they want!" Robin added.

We headed towards the door ready to fight whoever got in our way. When we got outside I noticed the girl that I beat down surrounded by three other girls. We walked with confidence in their direction as everybody started forming a circle around us to witness the second round of our fight. Just as we started to get close to them, Mike, Mont and Ty stepped in between us.

"What do you think you're doing?" Mike asked me.

"I'm about to beat her ass again!" I screamed loud enough for everyone to hear me.

Mike glanced over at Mont and Ty and said, "Can y'all please take them to the truck? I'll be right there."

I objected for a second until Mike shot me a look that made me change my mind immediately. As we started walking away I could see him hollering and pointing his finger in the face of the girl I was fighting. When he finally made his way to the truck he looked drained. Mike didn't say a word to any of us the entire ride to my house, so I kept quiet too. My thoughts were preoccupied with whether or not the girl I was fighting was one of his girlfriends or ex-girlfriends. The silence finally broke when we pulled up in front of my house.

"I don't think you should come in, because she's upset about the fight I had today with one of your girlfriends."

"She's not my girlfriend and I really need to talk to your mom."

When we all walked inside the house Momma Sue was sitting on the couch with her legs crossed, which alarmed us that she was pissed off.

"Right now is not a good time for company," she said in a calm manner.

"Can you please just hear me out for a second before we go?" Mike pleaded.

"Sure, speak what's on your mind."

"First of all, I don't think Keya deserves to go to the party because she got suspended from school."

At the sound of Mike's words, my heart and jaw dropped.

"The girl that she was fighting in school today is my sister Kelly. She has a real attitude problem because she's used to getting all the attention in school and being that Keya and her crew dresses real nice and gets a lot of attention, that drives her crazy. I constantly hear it at home, but I didn't think it would get to this point. I took care of the problem and I can promise you that there won't be any more trouble from either one of them," he spoke with confidence, now looking in my direction.

"How old are you?"

"I'm sixteen."

"You're very mature for your age. I appreciate you fixing the problem, because I don't condone them fighting in school. What did you say your name was?"

"Oh, I'm sorry. My name is Mike."

"Well Mike, you really put me at ease and I agree that Keya doesn't deserve to go to the party. I don't tolerate her getting in trouble and missing school. Being that it's not totally her fault though, you have my permission to come hang out and watch a movie with us. You can even pick the movie, unless you rather go to the party instead."

"I'll bring something to eat when I come. Just tell me what time."

"I like you already," Momma Sue said, putting everyone at ease. "Stop by around seven o'clock."

"Okay, I'll be here," Mike assured her, showing off his pearly whites.

Ty and Mont introduced themselves and was given permission to take Janet and Robin to the party. Janet was staying the weekend with us, so she was under Momma Sue's supervision. Of course she wrote down the address of where the party was taking place. When the fellas left, Momma Sue gave us a long lecture. We took in her every word and assured her that we would be more cautious in certain situations.

When the girl talk ended, Janet and Robin started getting ready for the party. They felt really bad about going without me, but I told them I was cool. I helped them get themselves together while filled with anticipation. I was anxious for Mike to arrive and spend some time with me. When my sisters were finally done getting ready, I jumped in my hot bubble bath and soaked for a while. I felt so relaxed as I laid back with my eyes closed. At that brief moment, I didn't have a worry in the world. Just when I was really beginning to enjoy my comfort, I started having flashbacks of my fight, but it was my mom's face. I was so into seeing her suffer in my thoughts, that I found myself punching the water. I hated her so much and I was glad she was in jail.

As I came out of my trance I noticed that there was water everywhere. It wasn't enough to cause a flood, but the walls and floor were drenched. My skin looked like it was starting to get wrinkled, so I lathered myself a few times with soap and got out. I put my hair in a ponytail and threw on some sweat pants and a t-shirt. By the time I got finish doing what I was doing it was only a little after six. Janet and Robin were about to leave and go eat with Mont and Ty first, so I stopped by Momma Sue's room to talk to her. When I knocked on the door and opened it, I realized

Mr. Damon was in the room with her. As I attempted to leave, Mr. Damon decided to get my undivided attention.

"Keya, I'm glad you're here. I need to talk to you for a minute."

I knew what it was about, but instead of trying to plead my case, I just took a seat at the foot of the bed and waited to hear what he had to say.

"Your mother told me about the fight that you had in school today."

Now was the time for me to plead my case, but before I could utter a word he cut me off.

"Before you start trying to explain, I want you to hear me out. Walk over to the mirror and take a good look at yourself. Do you see how beautiful you are?"

"Yes."

"Do you think that face was meant to be hit on?"

"No," I managed to say in my baby voice.

"The same goes for the girl you were fighting. If it ever comes down to you arguing with somebody and it possibly leading into a fight, be the bigger person and walk away. As long as nobody puts their hands on you there really shouldn't be a problem. Now if you don't agree with what I'm saying, we can get you a boxing or wrestling contract so we can make some money."

He made me feel a little better when he started laughing. His sense of humor is definitely what I needed at the particular moment. Momma Sue added her input once again before we went downstairs to wait for Mike to come.

I started to call and see if Mike was still at home or on his way, but I didn't want to seem desperate. A half an hour later the door bell was ringing. I intentionally jumped up from the couch and ran upstairs so Momma Sue could answer the door. She smiled at me knowing what I was up to. I went to the bathroom and checked myself out in the mirror to make sure I looked okay. A few strands of hair were out of place, so I took my pony tail out and did it all over again. When I was totally satisfied with my appearance, I slowly strutted down the steps like the princess that I am.

Upon entering the living room, Mike was sitting on the couch looking handsome. He got up and gave me a friendly hug, then handed me the movie. I went to go put the movie in, while Momma Sue went to get a knife to cut the steak and cheese calzones Mike brought for us to eat. The name of the movie was called Rain Man, featuring Tom Cruise, Dustin Hoffman and Jodie Foster. The movie was good, but the food was even better.

After the movie was over, Mike and Mr. Damon talked about sports while me and Momma Sue cleaned up. When everything was back to normal, they left me and Mike downstairs by ourselves, but I was certain Momma Sue would be lurking. I put another movie on the television, but we were so busy talking about a variety of things that I couldn't tell you what was on. One thing that I was sure of, was that time really does fly when you're enjoying yourself. We were so wrapped up in our conversation that we didn't hear or notice Janet and Robin come in the door. Me and Mike said our goodbye's, then he left with Mont and Ty.

"So how was the party?" I asked, not really interested.

"It was cool," Robin shared. "You know it definitely would've been better if you were there with us."

"It's always better when I'm there, because I'm the life of the party," I said sarcastically.

"You're so stuck on yourself," Janet told me.

"You got your nerve Jan. You taught me how to be this way."

"Okay, forget about that. Tell us about your day?" Janet said, switching the subject.

"It was cool. Momma Sue and Mr. Damon watched the movie Rain Man with us and we ate calzones. Overall, I had a great time. I'm hoping I can get off punishment tomorrow, but I doubt it."

"We'll stay in with you if we have to," Janet shared, before they both gave me a hug.

"Phone time!" I shouted, then made my way to the phone after they let me go.

Robin ran up to her room to call Mont and Janet called Ty from my room. I only got to talk to Mike for a few minutes because he had things to do in the morning. I got up to go check on Janet and Robin, who were sitting on my bed talking about the party. I joined in the conversation asking who was there and if any reckless eyeballs looked their way. When we finally went to sleep it was around four in the morning. None of us got up for breakfast, which naturally made Momma Sue come check on us.

"It sounded like y'all was having so much fun last night. I started to come join in," Momma Sue mentioned, before letting out a hearty laugh.

"You can hang with us tonight," I said in a low whisper.

"It sounds good to me. I'll see you sleepy heads later."

By the time I got out of bed it was close to one in the afternoon. Janet and Robin was still in my bed sleep with their mouths half open and I had no intentions on waking them up. Instead I got up to take

48

a shower. I stayed in there long enough to sing a few of my favorite songs.

The sleeping beauties finally woke up while I was getting dressed. While they got themselves together, I went downstairs and made us some bacon, eggs and toast. While we sat down and ate, we talked about new dance steps to add to our cheers. Janet put together a routine that was the bomb. We practiced the new moves for a few, and then we went to freshen up again so we could get ready to go to the movies with Momma Sue and Mr. Damon.

Instead of our regular movie night on Saturday's we went to go eat. Mr. Damon gave us a choice between Long John Silver's or Ponderosa. We all picked Long John Silver's except for Momma Sue, so we went to Ponderosa. The queen normally always had the final say. Either way we couldn't lose, but Long John Silver's was our first choice. I loved the salad bar at Ponderosa because it had wing dings and you could make your own ice-cream. We ate until our eyes practically popped out. I swear, we were so stuffed that we could barely move. Robin dropped her head to the table and Janet sat there constantly taking deep breaths. Momma Sue and Mr. Damon sat there and laughed at us for being so greedy.

Our food got a chance to digest a little bit and we finally were able to muster up enough energy to walk to the car. Mr. Damon threw in his Keith Sweat, Make It Last Forever cassette tape, which was my favorite and coasted down Ohio River Boulevard in his Lincoln Town car. The music was soothing, but it was too quiet in the car, so I decided to break the silence.

"Hey dad," I called out to his surprise.

"What's up Keya?" He finally managed to answer me.

"We been talking about you a whole lot lately and we would really love for you to move in with us."

"We won't take no for an answer,"Robin joined in.

"We sure won't," Momma Sue added, as she ran her fingers through his curly jet black hair.

"You have to say yes because you're stuck with us," Janet added, causing everyone to laugh.

"I guess that means yes," he responded.

We expressed to him how happy we were that his answer was yes. We all enjoyed the sounds of Keith Sweat the rest of the way home after everybody spoke their minds.

The rest of the day breezed on by. Since there weren't any chores for us to do, we jumped on the phones to call our boyfriends. Mike wasn't home, but I was totally caught off guard by how friendly his sister Kelly was with me, especially after the way I beat her down. She even called me Sis before we hung up.

Janet and Robin didn't have any luck either, which meant that they were probably somewhere together. We sat around and talked for a while, took turns doing each other's hair; and when we ran out of things to do we went to bed.

The next four days seemed to drag for me because I was still on punishment and suspended from school. My teachers did me a huge favor by sending my work home for me to do through Janet and Robin. That helped me kill a little bit of time. I usually slept during the day and stayed up all night thinking that would help time go by faster. It actually made things worse for me because I would always be up by myself. When I say that I was bored out of my mind, that's an understatement. I wrote love letters to Mike every night while I was on suspension and sent them to him through Robin. I also wrote letters to myself, Janet, Robin, Momma Sue and Mr. Damon. I even used all the free time that I had on my hands to communicate more with my younger brothers Kenny and Eddie.

Thursday had finally come and my punishment and suspension was finally over. So were those long boring days I had to endure. My heart was racing on my way to school, because it felt like my first day all over again. Another reason for me feeling so anxious was I could hang out with my boyfriend without Momma Sue and Mr. Damon around.

You couldn't tell me that I wasn't the cutest thing that ever graced the halls of Schenley High

School when I stepped off the school bus. It was springtime or at least the weather suggested that it was and I took the liberty of throwing on a red and blue Pierre Cardin velour sweat suit, with my high top Reeboks that had the double straps. To add to that, I had my fresh spiral curls in, my cute glasses that I bought from Foxy Gloxy and my big name earrings.
Along with looking and feeling like a million bucks, I could detect the envy. I didn't care though. As long as they kept their hands to themselves like Mr. Damon advised me, there wouldn't be any type of misunderstandings.

    I didn't get to see Mike until lunch, but when he greeted me with them sweet kisses that I loved, I wasn't even mad no more. Before I could even ask he told me that he had practice all weekend. I knew he was telling the truth because we had just won the city league championship in basketball and was going after the state crown. He walked me to my class and promised to call me after practice. I was a little disappointed because I had high hopes of spending time with him after being on punishment for almost a week, but I understood.

    During my last few classes of the day I daydreamed about the basketball team quickly winning the state championship. That way I could be with my boyfriend all the time. As I went further in my thoughts, the bell indicating the end of class interrupted me right before my visions of me and Mike having sex began to manifest. I was thankful that class was over, but I wanted to experience how good mental sex was. Still trying to capture that moment, I gathered all my belongings and headed towards my last period class.

I spotted the principal standing outside the door of my class with Mike's sister Kelly when I bent the corner and my antennas immediately went up. My first instinct was to turn around and walk the other way, but I decided against it. I attempted to walk pass them with no such luck coming. The principal stopped me in my tracks and informed our teacher that he was taking us with him. We walked slowly and quietly to his office, which made the suspense build up about what he planned on saying. When we finally reached our destination, he ordered us to sit down.

"You young ladies should be well aware of why you're here," he said, with a serious look on his face.

We both looked at each other slightly confused, then shrugged our shoulders. What we were sure of was that he was going to let us know.

"The both of you nearly caused a riot last week and I won't tolerate that happening again."

"You told us that three times on Friday," Kelly reminded him.

"Yeah Mr. Billups, every-."

"Well maybe I need to let y'all know three more times. If it happens again I won't hesitate to kick y'all out of my school. Do I make myself clear?"

"Before you rudely cut me off I was trying to tell you that everything is cool between us," I responded in a smart tone.

"I hope that's the truth," he said.

"That's my sister," I said to my own surprise. "You'll never have a problem out of us again."

"That's good to hear. Now is there anything else we need to discuss?"

The eye contact from the principal was now gone. He kept looking down constantly blinking as if something was in his eye. When we both expressed that we didn't have anything else to say, we were permitted to leave. As we reached the hallway, Kelly initiated the conversation.

"He could've said that to us in the hallway by our class. All he did was repeat the same stuff from Friday. His nasty ass just wanted to stare at our chest and between our legs. Did you see when he kept blinking real hard?"

"Yeah, I thought he had something in his eyes or something," I responded.

"When I saw his eyes locked in between my legs I shut them real fast," Kelly shared.

We were both laughing our hearts out as we entered the classroom. When everybody looked up at us, we knew we were being disruptive. I thought it was definitely going to get us a trip back to the principal's office. To avoid that from happening we both apologized to Mrs. Cooley and the class then took our seats. Instead of our regularly scheduled Phys. Ed. class last period, it was the second of an eight week class that we had to watch movies on different topics such as drugs abuse, alcoholism, safe sex, H.I.V., etc.... As I sat and watched I instantly began thinking about my poor excuse for a mother. All the stages that I watched the people on film go through; I had the unfortunate luxury of witnessing in my own household. I didn't realize a tear had fallen from my eyes until it hit the paper on my desk. I was relieved when the bell rung for class to end because I was getting more emotional by the second.

Me and Kelly were the first two people out the door. We picked up our conversation about the principal and shared a few more laughs as we exited the building. When I spotted Janet and Robin I headed in their direction.

"I'll see you tomorrow Sis," Kelly shouted, as she headed towards her friends.

"What was that about?" Janet asked in an agitated tone.

"What!" I replied, already knowing what she was talking about.

"How did y'all get so cool all of a sudden?" Robin intervened.

Janet and Robin wasn't pleased at all to see me walking with Kelly and especially hearing her call me her sister.

"It just happened," I answered honestly.

"Whatever," Janet responded, clearly upset with me.

I could understand where they were coming from. They didn't mind the fact that we settled our differences. It had always been just the three of us against the world and the thought of me befriending someone else didn't sit well with them. They didn't care about the fact that she was Mike's sister and how it was in my best interest to get along with her.

It took a little time, but they eventually opened up and embraced Kelly too. In a matter of time she became part of our inner circle. When she first started hanging with us we would tease her about being a spy for her brother and his boys, but those jokes quickly ended when she started messing with one of the football players.

Kelly had all the attributes to be a part of our crew. For one, she dressed fly, she was beautiful like us and weighing a hundred twenty-one pounds, she had all the right curves on her five foot frame to make the fellas drool. Her Anita Baker hairstyle only made her beauty stand out more. One of the most important things though, was that she was a member of the school cheerleading squad and loved cheerleading just as much as we did. Not only was she a part of the squad, she was also good friends with the captain of the cheerleading squad. Kelly spoke with her and she agreed to let us try-out. I heard through the grapevine that Melissa was a real bitch, but when I had the opportunity to personally meet her she seemed cool and down to earth. Melissa was also cute, with thick thighs and looks that sort of resembled Whitney Houston. She was a shade over five feet tall. During the audition, she was impressed with our confidence and skills. Furthermore, she concluded that cheerleading was what we were born to do.

After the try-outs were over, Kelly joined me, Janet and Robin on the floor and we did our own thing. We went raw with no beat, but we were accustomed to staying in rhythm from our claps.

"Try-out are over," one of Melissa's assistants blurted out.

We ignored her and continued to do what we did best. As we got into our routine everybody in the room gave us their undivided attention. When Melissa stepped up to the front to watch we really put on a show for her. Not only did we make the team, Melissa asked if some of our routines could be added to the cheerleading squads. It was an unbelievable feeling. Next to the basketball and football teams, the cheerleading squad was the hot topic in our school.

My sophomore year flew by traveling to road games and my relationship with Mike got more intense being that we were together all the time. In the beginning I thought he would feel awkward having me around all the time and grow tired of me. I always heard stories about all the cheating and extracurricular activities that went on and I automatically threw Mike in that category. I was wrong and it was a blessing that it all went smooth and the whole experience taught me that if I didn't trust my boyfriend, I shouldn't be with him. With that being said, I took the time to mentally connect with him more. As we got deeper into our relationship, my understanding about compatibility became extreme. That helped in a lot of ways mainly when I didn't get the opportunity to go to the prom with him his junior year. The trust was solidified even more after his mother made it clear to me that his prom date Lori was practically family. I was with him for the after prom and during his senior year I got the whole experience. All my girls went too, so it was like a big family reunion. We all looked fabulous, but Robin took the show winning Prom Queen. Up until that point Mike and I had never been sexually active. However, I knew that wouldn't last beyond prom night. As bad as I wanted to give myself to Mike, I was afraid that my past would come back to haunt me.

Later that night, my first real sexual experience was Heavenly. He took his time and the only thoughts I had were of loving him for the rest of my natural life. Janet, Robin and Kelly even got naughty that night.

After that first encounter we had sex at least four times a week for the next three months. Mike and his friends were attending the University of Michigan soon, so I wanted to have sex with him as much as I possibly could.

During our last week of sexual activities before he left for school, he convinced me to let him take the condom off. It was the best idea that he could've came up with. I must've exploded five times or more then I normally did. The incredible feeling was unexplainable. I never thought I could feel so good inside and out. I wanted to feel this way every single day. The day he left for college was one of the saddest days of my life. It felt like a part of me died. On top of that, my gut feeling told me that my fairy tale was coming to an end.

CHAPTER 2

My junior year was tough for me. Although me and my girls were still going strong on the cheerleading squad, the long distance relationship was taking its toll. If I was lucky I got to talk to Mike on the phone three times a week. He told me that class and football practices was taking up all his time, but he promised me that he'd start finding more time to call. I was hoping he kept his word, because I was feeling totally rejected. I was used to having sex all the time and now I wasn't getting it at all. I was mentally and emotionally losing it. I needed my man and I was seriously thinking about jumping on the greyhound bus to go stay with him for the weekend. When I called and told Kelly what my intentions were she got his dorm phone number for me so I could call and let him know I was on my way to visit. My heart was beating three times the normal pace as I dialed the number. On the forth ring a female's voice answered the phone.

"Stop it! Hello!" She answered through giggles.

"Can I speak to Mike please?" I asked in a polite tone, even though I was extremely agitated.

"Mike is very busy right now. Can I take a message?"

"Yes, you can. Tell him that Keya said get unbusy."

"You really think you're all that, don't you? How about watching your tone little girl."

"And who's going to make me?" I snapped out of frustration.

"I allowed you to spend time with him at the after prom, but I can arrange it to where you're a distant memory. Now you really need to watch your tone."

"Lori! You sneaky bitch!"

Before I could express myself the way I wanted to the phone went dead on the other end. I made several attempts to call back and give her a piece of my mind, but I kept getting a busy signal. I can't begin to describe how furious I was. I called Kelly to tell her about what happened.

"Get out of here! No she didn't!" Kelly said sounding surprised.

"She's dead wrong for that! They never messed around before. I swear to you, she just rode there with my dad and her dad to go visit Mike. She got a boyfriend, so I don't know what that was all about. Me and Mike look at her as our sister. We're like family with her family. I wouldn't have given you the number if something was going on with them."

"It just don't add up Kelly."

"What's that?"

"Why didn't Mike give me the number?" I questioned, barely able to hold back my tears.

"I can't answer that, but I'm sure he'll have a good reason."

"He better!"

I hung up with Kelly feeling even worse, so I told Janet and Robin about what happened.

"Mike wasn't there when you called. She was in the apartment with Mont and Ty. They told her to answer the phone because they were bringing their new couch in the house," Robin explained.

"And how do you know all that?" I inquired.

"Damn Keya! Do you think I would lie to you?" She asked, with a look on her face that could kill.

"I didn't say you were lying. I just wanted to know how you knew."

"Because Mont called and told me."

"What if he was covering up for Mike? You know they always stick together."

"He was definitely telling the truth. I heard her in the background telling him to stay out her business."

"Whatever," I said, ready to change the subject.

I believed Robin and decided to give Mike the benefit of the doubt. I was willing to wait for him to call and give me his version before I passed judgment on him. Two days went by and still not a word though. I laid in my bed with his varsity jacket on and cried my eyes out for the next five days. I went to school with bags under my eyes and I couldn't focus at all during my classes. The girls knew I was in a real funk when I barely showed up for cheerleading practice. I didn't want to do nothing but sit by the phone and wait for Mike to call. Either that or put my hands around Lori's throat.

Momma Sue normally stayed out of our teenage love episodes, but she figured enough was enough. She stopped by my room to talk to me about my depressed mood, but there was only so much she could do for me. I just wanted to be by myself. Early that Saturday morning I heard a knock on my door.

"Go away!" I shouted, with my face glued to the pillow.

When I heard the door open and then shut, I was hoping that whoever it was just peaked in, saw that I didn't want to be bothered and left. When I felt a hand touch my shoulder I took a deep breath and prepared to snap.

"Didn't I say go away! Just leave me alone! Please!"

"That's not the welcome I expected," Mike said, looking handsome as ever.

"Get away from me! You're lucky I don't have nothing close enough to throw at you!"

"Mont and Ty told me about the stunt Lori pulled, but I swear I don't know what that was about. Lori is like a sister to me."

"Yeah whatever! I haven't heard from you in a week!"

"I can explain why."

"I'm listening."

"The quarterbacks had to stay with the coaches for a week to study the playbook. We also had to study film."

I didn't believe one word he said, but lie or not, I was glad to have him in my presence. Umm, and when I tasted his sweet lips my whole attitude changed. I was under his spell, ready to do whatever he said.

"Go get dressed. I'll be downstairs waiting."

"Okay," I answered helplessly.

I jumped up, got in the shower and threw on some blue jeans, a t-shirt, leather jacket and a pair of tennis shoes. I quickly pulled my hair into a ponytail and was ready to go. When I came downstairs and saw Momma Sue, I could see the relief in her eyes.

"Thank you," she told Mike, while giving him a hug. "You have a good time baby," she whispered in my ear before she gave me a hug and a kiss on the cheek.

"I will," I assured her, with a slight smile on my face.

We went and ate lunch at Wanda's on the Hill, and then he took me to his cousin's shop to get my nails and feet done. It was a different experience for me because me and the girls usually did our own nails. Kelly never mentioned going to her cousin's shop to us, but I must admit, she was good at what she did. She cut the extra layer of skin and made my whole hand look flawless. She did the same with my feet. All the dead skin that she scraped off made them feel smooth. They felt so much lighter.

Our next stop was the art museum. Neither one of us really cared for art though. It was just somewhere we could walk around and hold hands. I had no complaints. I just wanted to be with him. An hour had gone by after one of the tour guides finished escorting us around. I found myself admiring some of the pieces we actually looked at. Where we ended up next was the icing on the cake. We made love for the rest of the day at Mike's parents' house. He was real gentle with me. Every sexual position you could imagine, we did it. When it was my turn to be dominant I rode his pony like there was no tomorrow. When I saw his eyes roll up in his head I knew I was putting my thing down. That moment was short lived, because Mike stole the show when he performed oral sex on me. I couldn't handle the way he devoured my kitten. With every thrust of his thick, long tongue I exploded all over the place. I shook uncontrollably and I don't think I stopped shaking until the next morning. Little did Mike know he was creating an animal.

My baby had our whole weekend planned out. We hung out and did a variety of things during the day, then we had wild, crazy sex all night. When he drove me to school that Monday morning, I was sad because he had to go back to school. He promised me that he would call me every single day during the week and come back home on the weekends. I was cool with our arrangements. We engaged in a long intense kiss, which helped energize me.

Later on that day me and the girls got together and talked about our weekend with our boyfriends. All of us had the feet and nail experience, but everything else differed.

Janet went bowling the first night out with Ty. On the second night they went to Mr. Pocket's and shot some pool.

Robin and Mont went to the movies their first night and the following day they did some volunteer work at Mont's Aunt's daycare center.

Kelly and Stan went on a boat ride the first day. The next day they went horseback riding.

Another thing that we had in common was how much we enjoyed the sex all weekend. Up until then, none of us wanted to admit how overwhelmed with stress we were without our significant others around. It showed during cheerleading practice though. We looked a mess, but after our amazing weekend, Melissa was happy to see the backflips and all the extra energy during our routines.

"You know, it's amazing what type of power and control men have over us," Melissa shared. "I just want all of you ladies to be careful and always remember that we have the true power. My mother use to always tell me that we're the most dominant species in the world and it took me a long time to understand exactly what she meant. She constantly preached that to me after my first boyfriend broke my heart. She told me that all my pain would be a major part of my growth. She also told me that life would come easier when I started loving myself unconditionally first. I just thought I'd share that, because I been where y'all are now."

Melissa was never the type to just open up like that, so we really didn't know how to take her comments. A lot of the girls were quick to say she was stressed out about something. Maybe it was because she was graduating this year and that she was sad about leaving us. I just did the smart thing, which was lock her every word in my memory bank.

Being that Mike kept his word and called me every single day, sometimes more than once, my week flew by. When I had the luxury of getting more than one call a day I was loving it. On one of the calls he had Lori on the phone with us.

"Keya, I got Lori on the phone," he warned me.

"Oh, Okay," I responded, wondering what good would come out of this conversation.

"Lori, you need to tell her the truth about that stunt you pulled," Mike ordered.

"What Mike! I don't know what you're talking about!"

"Stop playing! You disrespected my girl and tried to mess up our relationship! You need to fix that!"

"Find somebody else! She ain't all that no way!"

"Bitch I'm more than you!" I snapped.

"Not on your best day!"

"I'm beating your ass when I see you!" I continued.

"Be careful bitch, you might not like the results if you come trying me!"

"Both of y'all shut up!" Mike ordered.

When we obeyed his command, he kept pressing to resolve the situation.

"Lori, why did you do that when Keya called me? It has to be a reason why you have a problem with her."

"Her and them things she be with turned their noses up at me a few times."

I didn't respond to her smart remark because Mike was upset enough.

"I hated how they constantly walked around the school like their shit didn't stink. To me, Keya acted like she was too good for everybody because you're her boyfriend."

"First of all," I said, in a clam manner. "I walked around with confidence before I met Mike. I never noticed you to turn my nose up at you and we never held a conversation with each other until you went to the prom with Mike. All girls have attitudes, but I don't think I'm better than everybody else. There's no reason for you to be offended, because I don't have a problem with you."

"I may have over-reacted and if so, I apologize for my actions. Me and Mike are like family. I made all those comments up to get you mad. Mike didn't do nothing wrong."

"Thank you. Everything's cool."

"Mike, I'm sorry for all the trouble I caused bro."

"I wasn't mad at you. I told Twan you were cheating on him with Mont and Ty."

"What! Why would you do something like that?"

"Do I really need to answer that question?"

"Maybe not, but you need to call and tell him that you lied!"

"I'm just playing," Mike joked.

"Ool, you make me sick! I have to go. Keya, that'll never happen again and I hope you sincerely accept my apology."

"I accept. Thank you."

Mike drove home that Friday night, but I was under the impression that he was coming home on Saturday morning. When I got home from cheerleading practice Friday evening, I went to go take a shower before I ate. Mike scared the living daylights out of me when I opened my bedroom door. He was laying on my bed watching television.

"What are you doing here?" I asked, still in shock.

"Damn, I miss you too!"

"I didn't mean it like that baby. You just scared the mess out of me. I was expecting you to be here tomorrow morning like you told me."

"I was missing you so much that I had to come home a little early."

"Aw, that's so sweet. My Mikey missed me. Come here and give me a kiss."

He got up off the bed and walked towards me. As soon as our mouths were set to meet, he put his finger on his mouth and looked towards the door.

"Momma Sue ain't killing me. The most you can get out of me in this house is a quick peck and a hug. I'll never forget the look on her face when I first met her. Do you remember that time you got suspended for fighting Kelly?"

"How could I ever forget? That was the longest weekend of my life; besides that week you didn't call me."

"Damn Keya, I thought we got pass that?"

"We did get pass it. I forgave you, but the memory is still there."

"Now back to what I was saying. Your mom had this killer look on her face that was unexplainable."

"Don't tell me Mr. Tough Guy was scared."

"Not as scared as you were."

"What are you talking about?"

"I never said nothing to you, but while I was driving you home, I noticed that some of your nails were broken, or should I say shorter than the others. I thought it might've been from the fight, but none of them were chipped. I put two and two together once I saw your legs shaking uncontrollably. You were scared to death of Momma Sue, so you bit them off. I'm surprised you didn't piss on yourself."

"Shut up Mike! I wasn't scared!"

"Oh, you wasn't? Tell me what happened to your nails then?"

"I-I."

"Yeah, just like I thought. You were shaking so much the seats was vibrating as if I had the bass turned up on my car system."

"Shut up Mike! You make me sick sometimes! You think you know everything don't you?"

"Not at all. I just know you thought Momma Sue was about to put something on that ass."

"Just shut up and kiss me," I said, in between laughter. "It ain't happening baby." I wasn't playing about that."

"You're serious ain't you?"

"Dead serious. If you want a kiss that bad I'll be waiting for you in the car."

"Where did you park at? I didn't see the car when I came in."

"Momma Sue had it. I just heard somebody come in the house, so I'm guessing it's her. I'll be waiting for you so don't be long."

Before he could get out the door I was already downstairs. I gave Momma Sue a hug and faked a quick conversation. Everything went prefect because she was in a rush to leave with Mr. Damon. I said a silent thank you and walked out the door leaving Mike behind. When he finally made his way out the door I was right there waiting for my kiss. It never failed, he always melted me with those sweet kisses of his.

During our ride to go get something to eat, I was in a daze thinking about the long conversations me and the girls had about getting our coochie ate. We wanted to know what we could do to please them back. With that being said, me and Robin snuck in Momma Sue's room and grabbed one of the porno flicks they had. It was the only way for us to get some general knowledge of what to do. We only watched and studied the flicks when Momma Sue and Mr. Damon weren't home, unless we watched them over Janet's house. In this one particular flick there was a man getting extra pleasure from getting his dick sucked. The part that confused us was how the women constantly went up and down without biting their dicks. Kelly made a suggestion about buying pickles to practice on. It seemed like an excellent idea so we did just that. Kelly and Robin caught on quick, but me and Janet bit our fair share of pickles before we got it right. I was brought out of my daze when Mike yelled in my ear.

"Are you okay?"

"Yeah, I'm cool."

"You were out of it for a minute. What were you thinking about?"

"Nothing really."

"You were thinking about something. I called your name about five times before I leaned over and yelled in your ear."

"I was thinking about how miserable I was when you didn't call me."

"I thought we-."

"Okay, okay, I'm just playing. I was thinking about the last time we had sex. When you licked and sucked on my pussy."

"Did you like it?"

"Are you kidding me? I loved it baby."

"That's good. I might be nice and give you another treat tonight."

I remained quiet while he continued to talk with his chest poked out. Little did he know, I had a big surprise of my own in store for him. I just had to focus on taking my time until my nerves calmed down. Once I gained control of the situation he'd be at my mercy, just like it took place on the porno flicks we watched. I couldn't wait for the night to unwind so I could experiment a little.

We ate at this greasy spoon restaurant on the Southside. It was much to my dislike, but I just sat there and nibbled on my food, trying to hide my displeasure from Mike as much as I could. When I finally looked up at him, he was sitting there shaking his head laughing at me.

"What?" I asked, trying not to blush.

"You're sitting there fighting with that food knowing you don't like it."

"I do like it."

"This food is nasty as hell and you know it."

"Well baby, it's the thought of you trying to feed me that counts."

"The thought my ass. This food is horrible. I can't wait to curse Ty out for recommending that I bring you here. Come on we're leaving."

He paid for our food, but not without expressing how he felt about the food. Both of us were still hungry, so I took the liberty of treating him to McDonald's. I ordered a double cheeseburger, small fries and a small orange drink. Mike's greedy ass ordered a Big Mac, fish sandwich, large fries, large drink and a hot fudge sundae. It was a good thing I was good at saving money, because feeding Mike could be expensive. I told him that was the last time that I would offer to fork the bill.

After we gobbled down our food, we met up at the local night spot at Manchester Elementary School. Well actually, everyone called it night gym. It's where all the fellas and younger kids played basketball at. While they ran up and down the court trying to be Michael Jordan, me and my girls huddled up and strategized about the surprises our men were in store for. Kelly's hot ass had already beat everybody to the punch by doing her thing before they came to the gym. She excitedly told us about how he moaned and groaned with lust and pure pleasure. As she continued to fill us in, Ms. Kelly lit up like a Christmas tree with the bright smile she displayed. From her expression and the way she expressed herself, we could tell she enjoyed herself.

"I'm telling y'all, being able to please him back made the sex so much better."

We quickly ended our conversation when my brothers Kenny and Eddie walked over towards us.

"Damn! Y'all look good," Edde flirted.

"Boy you better sit your butt down somewhere before I lay you across my knee and spank you," Janet teased.

"Yeah right. You know you in love with me. I can tell by the way you smile at me."

"Come here?" Janet requested, as she reached out for him. "I can't, my other girlfriend is over there watching me."

"Boy you don't have a girlfriend," I added.

"Yes I do, but Uncle Greg been trying to call you so he can give you your money."

"I'll call him tonight."

"He said your phone is always busy."

"I do be on the phone all the time. What time do y'all have to be in the house?"

"At eight o'clock. Can you drive us home so we can stay out and play a little longer?"

"Go ask Mike and see what he says."

Kenny ran straight on the basketball court and interrupted the game that was in heated battle, just to ask Mike if he could take them home.

"Get off the court little man!" A few guys shouted out.

"Yo, he cool y'all! That's my lil' brother," Mike told them.

"Kenny, you can't be running on the court like that man. What if somebody accidentally knock you over and you get hurt?"

"I'm sorry Mike. I was just coming to ask you if you could take us home so we can stay out a little later?"

Mike nodded his head yes, then playfully shoved him off the court. He ran over to let me know Mike said yes and ran over to the other side of the gym where the younger kids were playing basketball. Just sitting there watching my brothers play made me think about Momma Sue and how she treated them like they were her sons. When me, Robin and Janet outgrew hanging out with her and Mr. Damon, Eddie and Kenny took our place. They even spent the night with us from time to time. Mr. Damon loved taking them to the Pirates, Penguins and Steelers games. They even went to go see Pro Wrestling events when they came to town.

Mike was crazy about my brothers too. During the ride home the three of them were so caught up into themselves that I felt totally ignored. I was a little upset at first, but then I realized that I'd have Mike's undivided attention soon. Mike wanted to stay and spend a little more time with them, but after my hour long conversation with my Uncle Greg it was time to go. As we pulled up in the back of his parents' house,

I decided to make my move. I grabbed at his crouch and rubbed it gently until I felt his stiffness. As I unzipped his pants and pulled out his manhood, his eyes got big as pool balls. I made sure my mouth was nice and wet before I went to work. I teased him by slowly licking on it. I then deep throated the dick, altering my pace. I kept my mouth open as wide as I could and continued to go up and down, occasionally licking the tip of his dick where it was extra sensitive at. Mike started making all these crazy noises and speaking languages I never heard before. There was one sound that I was familiar with and when that loud groan came I knew I had to pull away before he exploded. When my mission was completed I looked at him with a devilish grin and waited until he caught his breath so he could speak.

"Damn! Where the fuck did that came from?" He asked.

"As good as you made me feel, as you always make me feel, I had to do something. The way you licked and sucked on me, how could I cheat on you?"

"We need to go in the house so we can finish," he told me. It was more of a demand.

"I'm not ready to go in the house yet. I want to do it in the car."

"Stop playing girl, you got me horny. Let's go in the house."

"I'm serious baby. I want to do it in the car."

I had to do a few things to persuade him and show him that I was serious, but it didn't take too long for him to get the message. We began snatching away at each other's clothes and before I knew it we were in the back seat of the Lincoln Town car getting busy. He had my feet propped up against the back of the headrest, parting my legs enough for him to get between them. He hit the bottom of my ocean with every stroke causing me to moan with pleasure. The louder I moaned, the harder he pounded. In the end we moaned in harmony as if singing on tune like R & B singers. Unintentionally we fell asleep naked in the back seat.

The following morning we woke up from a knock on the window. To our surprise it was Lori. She shook her head with a slight grin on her face, holding a blanket in her hands. I panicked for a second because I was embarrassed, but I quickly got it together. I hit the locks and grabbed the blanket from Lori, making sure she couldn't get a good look at Mike in the nude. After I covered us up she hopped in the passenger's seat.

"I bet that was fun," she said, with that same grin on her face.

"You don't have nothing else better to do?" Mike asked.

"That's not the way to treat the help now is it bro?"

"Don't make me go in the house and call Twan," he threatened.

"I put my thing down last night, so he might not have enough energy to pick up and answer the phone. Whenever you do talk to him make sure you give him a few tips about sex in the car so we can try it. Well lovebirds, I have to go, sorry I can't stay and talk. Oh and by the way, Keya I'm envious of that smile you're displaying and I hope to go through that experience and have one similar to yours."

I guess it was evident the way I felt about my wild and adventurous night, but I wasn't trying to hide it anyway. Momma Sue always told us that there wasn't nothing wrong with loving someone as long as they loved you back and I knew Mike loved me. We slid on our clothes and he dropped me off at home.

Robin and Janet were in the kitchen fixing brunch but before I joined them I went to take a quick shower.

"Are you going to tell us or what?" Janet asked when I came and sat down.

"Am I going to tell you what?" I teased.

"Don't play with me girl!"

"Why can't you go first?"

"I'll go!" Robin shouted. "I wanted to wait for what I thought was the perfect moment, so I waited until we woke up early this morning when Mont was nice and hard. It feels like it was a great performance too. After he squirted all over the place he wanted to have sex, but I demanded he bring me home. I swear he begged and pleaded until his eyes started watering and it took everything inside of me not to give in. I quickly gave him a peck when we pulled up in front of the house and jumped out the car without making eye contact with him. Eager as he was tonight should be something special."

"I basically did Ty after he did me. He was definitely surprised and when I really got into it he was at my mercy. I wish y'all could've seen me at work. He's probably on his way to come back and pick me up right now," Janet said with a devilish smile.

"Well my night was a little different," I stated, with a huge smile on my face. "After we dropped Eddie and Kenny off we pulled up in the back of his house. That's where I made my move at. First, I got him nice and hard, then I started working my magic. I threw it in my mouth, deep throated it and licked on the tip until he went crazy. After we finished up in the backseat we ended up falling asleep. Y'all won't believe who found us sleeping naked."

"Who?" They both asked at the same time.

"Lori. She knocked on the window and brought us a blanket to cover up with."

"Stop lying!" Janet told me.

"I swear I'm not lying. She woke us up and that's when I came home just now to take a shower."

"Anybody could've came and seen y'all," Robin added.

"You're right, but that comes with the thrill of being spontaneous," I said, with an innocent smile.

We talked a little more about our wild adventures, and then I went upstairs to take a nap. I was still a little tired from the night before and the pancakes, sausage and eggs that I ate had me stuffed. While I was asleep, I had a dream of a fairytale wedding. I didn't have a clear vision of where me and Mike got married at, but well over three hundred people attended. Me and the bridesmaids wore all white, while Mike and the guys wore white with sky blue trimming. Before we got the opportunity to say our vows an unknown female objected to the pastor about us getting married. She said that we shouldn't get married because her and Mike were having a baby together. I woke up in a sweat, looking around for the mysterious woman, but had no such luck of locating her. I kept telling myself that it was just a dream and I eventually went back to sleep.

When Mike came to pick me up later on that day I told him about the crazy dream I had. I definitely didn't get the reaction that I expected from him though. A slight smirk formed on his face, but for the most part he was nonchalant about it and that made me mad. I punched him hard on the shoulder so that he would focus on me.

"Did you hear what I told you about my dream?"

"Yeah I heard you, but you didn't have to punch me to get me attention."

"I had to do something!"

"Not that!"

"Is that all you have to say?"

"Are you serious? What the fuck do you want me to say? It was a dream! Your dream! It wasn't real!"

"Well it felt real," I said, looking for a little sympathy.

"Most dreams do feel real until we actually wake up. You're wide awoke now, so let it go."

"What if I don't want to?"

"Grow up Keya!"

"You know what, just take me home! You get on my nerves!"

I was expecting him to go back and forth with me for a second and then let me have my way, but he made a few turns and headed back towards my house. I was at my boiling point, but I held it together because I didn't want him to see that he won.

"Can you please drop me off at Janet's house instead?" I asked in a calm manner.

He didn't say a word or look in my direction. In fact, he turned up the music and kept his eyes glued to the road. When we got to Janet's house he pulled over and kept the music playing loud. I started to turn it down and speak my mind, but I got out and slammed the door behind me. Mike hated when I slammed his door and I could feel his eyes cutting through me as I walked away. When I heard his tires screeching I knew he was mad.

When I stormed through Janet's door Ty was in the living room sitting on the couch with her.

"Oh I'm sorry. I didn't know you were here Ty."

"Why not, she's irresistible. Where Mike at? He told me he was picking you up."

"We had an argument and I had him drop me off."

"What was y'all arguing about that he had to drop you off?" Janet asked, finally breaking her silence.

"I was telling him about the crazy dream that I had. We were about to get married and this chick, that I never saw before told everybody that was there Mike shouldn't marry me because she was having his baby. He basically didn't pay me no attention while I was telling him about it and I got mad."

"Keya, what did you really expect him to say?" Ty asked, defending his boy.

"I don't know. Maybe I just wanted him to tell me that it wasn't true and that it'll never happen. I wasn't trying to start an argument with him, I love Mike."

"I know you do," Ty told me. "Don't worry I'll fix it."

Seconds later, he picked up the phone and paged Mike. After he was done we sat there in silence anticipating Mike's call. About fifteen minutes later the phone rang. Ty attempted to pick it up and answer it, then caught himself. We both looked over at Janet and waited for her to answer it. She let it ring one more time before she decided to pick it up.

"Hello. Oh she's not home right now Mrs. Woods, but I'll let her know you called. Okay, you have a good day too."

When Janet hung up the phone we sat in silence again waiting for the phone to ring. Ty broke us out of our silent state by cracking jokes. He talked about people on the cheerleading squad, the basketball and football teams. He even had a few things to say about a few of the teachers. We were laughing so hard that we didn't hear the phone ringing. When Janet rushed over to answer it, the ringing stopped. As soon as she attempted to come back over towards us the phone began to ring again. She answered it, then handed it to Ty.

"What's up man?"

"I wish I knew," Mike said, sounding dry on the other end.

"We're about to go to the movies. Swing by and come with us," Ty suggested.

"I'll pass. Keya might start acting crazy again. She was snapping at me about a dream she had."

"I know. She told me and Janet all about it. I understand where both of y'all coming from. Keya just feels a little insecure because you're not around her all the time like you use to be. It shouldn't hurt to tell your girl what she wants to hear sometimes so she won't feel that way. Some people believe that their dreams really do come true."

"You're right T. I'm on my way back over there, but don't tell her that I'm coming."

"I understand man and I wish it didn't have to be that way. Are you sure there's nothing that'll change your mind about coming with us?"

"He said no didn't he?" I asked Ty after he hung up the phone.

Ty gave me a sad look and tried to change the subject. I started to question him again, hoping that his response would be different, but when he threw his head in his lap that pretty much told me everything I needed to know.

"Janet, let's go upstairs for a second?" Ty asked.

"No, my Sis is here. You always being nasty boy. Just wait until I make sure my Sis is cool and I'll take real good care of you afterwards."

"Girl stop playing! That ain't why I want you to go upstairs!"

"Go ahead I'm cool. If I can't find nothing on t.v. I'll just walk home."

"Don't go nowhere, we won't be that long," Ty told me.

He smacked Janet on her butt as they walked towards the steps. I don't know why, but I felt a little envy as I watched them walk up the stairs. When they disappeared out of my sight I began to feel lonely. I wanted to page Mike and apologize to him, but my stubborn self would rather suffer mentally and emotionally instead of patching things up with my man.

I got up to go surf through the t.v. channels, but the doorbell stopped me in my tracks. I didn't recall Janet saying anything about expecting more company. Maybe it was Robin or Kelly stopping by because they had a problem with their boyfriends as well. Wow, I can't believe I just went there. It's sad when you're so miserable that you want everyone else around you to feel the same way you do. When I opened the door I had to rub my eyes to make sure I wasn't seeing things.

"Yeah it's me," he said with a straight face.

"Baby I'm sorry," I said with excitement as I wrapped my arms around his neck and started kissing him.

"I'm sorry too. I should've handled the whole situation differently."

"That's over with," I told him. "I just want to leave and go with you. Oh, I have to let Janet know I'm leaving."

"They already know I was coming to get you."

"That's why they went upstairs all of a sudden."

Mike scooped me up off my feet and carried me to the car. We drove around for a little bit, going nowhere in particular. Mike did what all the guys that drove did. He rode through all the neighborhoods around the city. He constantly stopped to talk to people he knew, but I think he intentionally did that to show everybody how his girl complimented his interior. I gracefully represented for him by displaying a bright smile on my face looking cute as ever, while messing with the stereo system. When the rain started coming down we continued to drive around enjoying each other's company. My baby looked so good and I wanted to eat him alive right then and there. I let my heart rate settle down, then I threw my head in his lap as he continued to drive. I whipped his joystick out and began to munch on it as if it was my first meal in days. I felt him tightening up, but the only thing on my mind was watching his hose spray. Before I could get my wish the car came to a complete stop and he pushed me up.

"Come on, get out the car," he demanded.

"Are you crazy? It's pouring down raining out there."

Instead of acknowledging anything I said he got out the car. I stared at him as if he was crazy for a second, then against my better judgment I got out and followed him. I couldn't believe I was really doing this. It was raining so hard that I could barely see. Mike picked me up and sat me on the trunk of the car, pulled my pants down to my ankles, and then he ate my pussy so good that I thought I was going to have a heart attack. The rain didn't seem to be a problem anymore. The harder it poured down on us, the more enhanced my hormones became. After I sprayed like a skunk he let me down off the trunk. I thought it was over until he bent me over and pounded me from behind. My legs started feeling rubbery, but the way he had me locked in I knew I was safe and that I wouldn't fall. The deeper he drove himself into me, the louder my moans got. I knew he was ready to explode because he started pumping faster and faster. He eventually stopped pounding, but he held me real tight, while still holding his stiffness deep inside me.

"Are you done yet baby?" I asked, no longer able to feel my legs.

"Shh, be quiet for a second. Don't move," he ordered in a whisper.

A few seconds later he pulled his limp dick out of me and we got back in the car. We were soak and wet, dripping all over the place, but the experience that I just had was well worth it. He sped home so we could get out of our wet clothes and after a nice hot shower together we cuddled and watched movies that we rented from Blockbuster for the rest of the night.

The rest of the weekend went well, but when the morning came for him to leave something felt strange. I didn't know exactly what it was, but I could feel it. I grabbed all the clothes that he wore over the weekend and took them home to wash them. Before I threw his things in the washing machine I checked all of his pockets to make sure there wasn't anything in them. To my surprise, I found a piece of paper with the name Stacia on it; along with a phone number underneath the name. I told myself that's what I must've been feeling. Maybe Stacia was the female in my dream. I couldn't believe this was happening to me. I couldn't sit down, so I started pacing back and forth in my room. My heart began to race rapidly as I closed my door so I could use the phone in private. I dialed the phone number on the paper and a female answered.

"Hello, may I speak to Stacia?" I asked, trying to hide the anger in my voice.

"This is her."

"This is Mike's sister. He told me to call and let you know that he can't call you anymore because he has a girlfriend."

"I'm sorry, but there must be some type of misunderstanding. Hold on for a second please. Mike, come get the phone!"

"Who is it?" He asked.

"She said she's your sister, but that's not Kelly on the phone."

"Give me the phone. Who is this?"

"What the fuck is going on!" I snapped. "You told me that you were on your way back to school this morning!"

"Keya, I am. Hold up, let me explain. I had to come-."

Before he could finish his sentence, I slammed the phone down in his ear. I avoided all his calls for a few weeks and I avoided Kelly too. After about a month he finally gave up. It was difficult trying to get over my first and only love, but when I constantly replayed Melissa's words of wisdom it helped me stand firm on not picking up the phone to call Mike. Although I continued to avoid him throughout the summer something deep inside told me that I would never be the same.

CHAPTER 3

    The summer of 92 was crazy for me, especially without having Mike as my boyfriend. Robin and Kelly were still going strong in their relationships and they both had gotten pregnant. I thought that Momma Sue and Mr. Damon would go bananas, but they were the total opposite. Both of them made it clear to Robin that it was important for her to stay focused on school, while they took care of the baby.

    Robin and Kelly spent most of their time in the house or with their boyfriend's so I spent a lot of time with Janet when she wasn't with Ty. I had my driver's license, so Mr. Damon would allow me to drive his car from time to time. The place to hang out was on the Hill, also known as the Hill District. It was so much to do on the Hill. There were basketball games damn near every day and everybody came out with their Sunday's best on to watch the festivities. Sometimes the day would end in violence, mainly because gangs were really starting to evolve throughout the inner city of Pittsburgh. The guys that didn't commit to gangs were drug dealers and plenty of drama came with that too.

    On this particular hot and sunny day I had on my Daisy Dukes, a wife beater and sandals to show off my pedicure. To add to the equation my hair was looking fabulous. I saw a whole lot of guys who gazed seductively in me and Janet's direction, but there was only one guy bold enough to approach us. He went by the name Slim. I must admit, Slim had a chizzled upper body and nice legs. I really couldn't tell how he got the name Slim. I figured maybe he was a small guy when he was younger or something. Slim wasn't shy at all though. He walked up to me and placed my hand in his before he started talking.

"I need to hurry up home and apologize to my mother," he said out of nowhere.

"Excuse me," I responded, totally puzzled from his comment.

"I don't mean to confuse you cutie. It's just that my mom use to always tell me about you when I was younger."

"Boy please! Your mom don't even know me!" I said, snatching my hand away.

"You're absolutely right."

"What are you talking about then?" I asked, still agitated.

"She told me that I would meet and instantly fall in love with a real angel and I never believed her until now. In my dreams I've been searching for you all my life."

Although he was corny, I thought it was sweet of him to put me in the same category as an angel. I respected his courage to approach me the way he did, so I decided to indulge in a conversation with him. Slim turned out to be pretty smart and I found myself enjoying his company. We ended up exchanging phone numbers after talking for over an hour.

During the next two weeks me and Slim talked on the phone at least three times a day. I finally had the opportunity to have a sit down with Kelly and when she proved to me that Stacia was their cousin I was highly upset with myself. I was filled with so much rage and regret because I didn't give Mike a chance to explain himself. At that moment I wished that I could turn back the hands of time, but I couldn't. The fact that he was away in college made me feel insecure about him being with someone else, so that was what put a major strain on our relationship.

The more I communicated with Slim, the more intrigued I became with him. With all the phone conversations and the intensity of the conversations, I finally felt comfortable enough to hang out with him. He picked me up in his customized Monte Carlo and took me on a tour of the Hill District. After making about ten stops, he drove to Elmore Square where we entered an apartment building. Once I stepped foot in the apartment I realized it was decorated to perfection. It was a living quarter made for a bachelor. When Slim locked the door behind us he dropped two bags of money on the couch and asked me to count it for him while he took a shower. My eyes lit up at the sight of all the money, I was even more impressed that he trusted me with it. It definitely made me let my guard down.

I counted a little over nine thousand dollars, which I stacked neatly on the coffee table. He came out of the bathroom with a towel wrapped around him exposing his muscular chest.

"How much was it?" He asked.

I was so busy analyzing his anatomy that I didn't hear him talking to me. He tapped me on my shoulder a few times until he finally got my attention.

"Keya!"

"Huh."

"Is everything okay?"

"Yeah, I'm good."

"Are you sure?"

"I'm positive."

"How much money was it?"

"Oh, it came up to nine thousand and six hundred dollars."

"Take three hundred out for yourself. Oh, and thanks baby."

"Thank you," I said as he planted a soft kiss on me.

As he walked towards his room to get dressed I grabbed the money he gave me and put it in my purse. I started to follow him in his room because I was extremely curious and horny. Nevertheless, I didn't want to seem easy. I held my composure and sat there in silence, waiting for him patiently. Ten minutes later he came out his room. Damn! He was looking so good with his waves spinning.

"You could've turned on the T.V. or something if you wanted to."

"I'm cool."

"Are you ready to go then?"

It took every ounce of strength that I had to say yes. I wanted to strip naked and tell him to come get it.

"Whenever you are," I fought myself to say.

We went and got some chicken wings on Centre Avenue, then sat in the car while we ate. Slim had all types of strange looking people running up to his car. The looks on their faces reminded me of my mother, which made me feel uncomfortable. I couldn't figure out what he was giving them, but whatever it was, it was in small balloons. Each person he handed a balloon to gave him money afterwards. I had seen enough and quickly asked Slim if we could leave.

"Yeah, I just have to take care of one more thing first."

He grabbed a pouch out of the glove compartment and got out the car. I watched as he walked over to a police car and discreetly handed one of the officers the pouch. Slim stood there and conversed with them for a few minutes, then as he walked off he started talking to everyone in the vicinity, which was now beginning to irritate me. He must've sensed my impatience because he headed towards the car in a hurry.

"Sorry about that," he said, as he jumped in the driver's seat. "It be real busy for me this time of day."

"Well you need to find a different time to come get me then!" I spat with frustration.

"Who the fuck do you think you're talking to!" He asked in an aggressive tone, gripping the back of my neck real tight.

"Stop it! You're hurting me!"

"I didn't mean to hurt you, but I don't ever want you to talk to me like that again. Do you hear me?"

"Yeah I hear you! Now can you please take your hand off me!"

When he finally released his grasp and dropped me off at home, I thought to myself; this should be the last time I affiliate myself with Slim. Although I was taken aback by what he had done, my loneliness caused me to overlook the red flags. I continued seeing Slim and the worse mistake that I ever made was having sex with him. For some reason, when you have sex with a guy he becomes controlling and over possessive like a woman is a piece of property that he owns. Don't get me wrong the sex was excellent, but he became very abusive when we started having sex. He beat on me for the pettiest reasons and sometimes for nothing at all. When I wasn't with him I was forced to stay in the house so that he knew where I was at all times. I got tired of sitting in his apartment alone all the time, so I decided to call my sisters to come pick me up so we could go watch the basketball games.

As we made our way through the crowd the look in Janet's eyes scared the mess out of me. They told me that something was terribly wrong. It wasn't long before I felt somebody grab me by my hair and slam me to the ground. It was Slim and he started kicking and punching on me while calling me crazy names for everyone to hear.

"Bitch! Didn't I tell you to stay in the fuckin' house! You'll learn to do what the fuck I tell you!"

He kept punching and stomping me until all my sisters jumped on him. I was so embarrassed. There had to be at least three hundred people looking at us. My lips were bleeding and I could feel my face blowing up like a balloon. My ribs and legs were also aching. When me and my sisters headed towards the car to leave, Slim stopped me before I got in.

"Keya wait, I need to talk to you for a second. I swear I didn't mean to put my hands on you baby. I promise you it won't happen again. Come home with me so we can talk about it."

"There ain't nothing for us to talk about. I'm tired of you putting your hands on me."

"She ain't going nowhere with you!" Janet shouted in a heated passion.

"You need to mind your fuckin' business!"

"And if I don't! Are you going to jump on me next you coward!"

"Keep pressing your luck bitch!"

"Your mother's a bitch!"

"It's cool Sis. I'll be okay," I said with my head hung low. I was too ashamed to look any of my sisters in the eyes, plus I didn't want Momma Sue and Mr. Damon to see me like this.

"You so stupid!" Janet responded in a hostile tone.

They got in the car and drove off. As soon as they were out of my sight I regretted not leaving with them. I got in the car with Slim and we rode straight to his apartment. I expected to hear an apology from him, but instead he sat on the couch, pulled out a folded bill and began snorting white power in his nostrils. I went to the bedroom, got undressed, then hopped in the tub. He came in there with me shortly afterwards.

"Hurry up and get out the tub!" He demanded.

"Why don't you just leave me alone!"

"What did I tell you about talking to me like that!" He snapped, grabbing a handful of my hair once again.

"You don't scare me! If hitting on me makes you feel like a man go ahead!"

"Bitch don't test me!"

"You heard what I said!"

He eventually left out the bathroom, but I noticed how he could barely keep his eyes open. I stayed in the tub and soaked for another half an hour hoping that he went back outside. The water was starting to get cold so I got out. My body was aching badly. It was a pain that I couldn't describe. I fought through it as I cleaned out the bath tub. When I finally took some time out to look in the mirror and groom myself I was horrified. I stormed out the bathroom to see if he was still in the house. I was determined to give him a piece of my mind, even if it meant going through it all over again. When I made my way to the living room, I found him on the couch snoring. I grabbed the phone and took it with me to the bedroom so I could call Janet to come get me.

"Did he put his hands on you again?" She asked out of concern.

"No I'm cool. Just hurry up though."

After I hung up the phone I began to search the house for the weapons he had. I came across a gun that was hidden under some t-shirts and an axe handle in the living room. I went in the bedroom to use the phone again. This time I dialed 911.

"I need help please," I whispered in a nervous tone. "My boyfriend is trying to beat me up again and I'm scared."

"Just tell me where you are and I'll send help right away."

"I'm at 1333 Elmore Square. Oh, the door number is four. Can you please hurry?" I asked, as I hung up the phone without getting a response.

Being that the police station wasn't too far away, I had to work fast. I grabbed the two shoe boxes full of money that he had hidden in the closet and dumped it all in my purse. As for the drugs, I left them where they were. Out of total frustration because of what he did to my face, I grabbed the axe handle and hit him so hard in his knee that I felt the vibration go through my body. The blow woke him up immediately. Before he knew what hit him I smashed his other knee. He tried to get up, but he fell to the floor hollering in excruciating pain. I looked him dead in his eyes and hit him one more time across his face.

Satisfied with the results, I messed up my hair, grabbed my purse, then I ran out the door screaming for help. Janet was coming up the steps as I was running out, but I ran pass her and threw my purse in the car. I then sat down in front of the building and began shaking uncontrollably. When the police finally arrived, I put on my best act and made myself seem hysterical. I answered all questions that I was asked, then I was taken to the hospital to have my injuries looked at. Besides from the bruised ribs I had, I would be back to normal in a few weeks. Slim was the unlucky one though. His kneecaps were shattered and to add to his problems, the police found the drugs and the gun. He got off without any legal drama because he had the person who's name the apartment was in take the charges. I still pursued the charges that I filed against him and he only received five years' probation. I wanted him to rot in jail, but things don't always work the way we want them to.

After being confined to a wheelchair and crutches for four months, Slim made a full recovery. He frequently rode pass my house and around my neighborhood making threats about his money. I think the fact that I put him in the hospital and broke up with him had a lot to do with it. His pride was in the way. He couldn't prove if I was the one who took the money or the police who searched his house. I knew what he was capable of though, so I wouldn't go any further than the porch if I wasn't with someone who could defend me. We called the police about Slim harassing me, but they said that he wasn't doing anything illegal by riding through the neighborhood. I didn't know what to do. I thought about just giving him his money back, but I knew he would still harass me. The best decision I came up with was to just sit on the porch and cry my eyes out.

I was totally caught off guard when Mont brought Mike with him to see his daughter. Initially he kept walking when he saw me, but turned around and sat down beside me. I didn't know what to say to him, so I remained quiet, staring out into the streets.

"How are you?" He asked, with a concerned look on his face.

"I'm okay."

"You don't have to lie to me. I know you, remember."

"All too well," I said, covering my face up with my hands.

"A lot of what you went through or what you're going through is my fault. I should've made you listen to me so you would've known Stacia was my cousin. I would still have you if I did."

"You can't blame yourself for the decisions that I made."

"Yes I can. There wouldn't have been no decisions to make if I would've just-."

"Just stop Mike, please! We can't take away what happened. I just want to move on and put all that stuff behind me."

"I understand," He said, staring at the ground, then he shifted his big brown eyes and stared at me.

Mike gently placed his lips on mines and we began to kiss. I just closed my eyes and savored the moment. It felt like old times all over again. Damn! I missed Mike so much. We sat and talked for a few hours before he left with Ty.

Over the next couple of weeks, me and Mike started spending a lot of time together. He told me that he wanted to be with me as much as he could before he went back to school and I was all for it. Sitting on the porch apparently became boring to Mike and he convinced me to start hanging out with him.

One evening me and my sisters decided to hang out with our boyfriends like old times. To our surprise the fellas wanted to go skating. When we arrived at Spinning Wheels it was jam packed. There were a handful of people skating that we knew from school, but other than that, the majority of the people were total strangers. We got in line to grab some skates, then we hit the floor.

It was evident that there were still things to learn about Mike, because I had no idea he could skate so well. Our little cute step we did was nothing compared to the line they formed. After a few times around, I started feeling dehydrated. I broke off to go get me something to drink. As I was standing in line I felt a hand aggressively grab me by the arm. The grip was so tight that I could barely feel my fingertips.

"I've been looking all over for you! You been hiding from me huh!"

"Get off my arm Slim!" I shouted, hoping to cause a scene.

"Shut the fuck up!" He hissed through clenched teeth. "I'm doing all the talking! If you want me to make a scene in here I will, but either way you're coming with me! Get your ass over there and put your shoes on! Let's go, because if I have to tell you again you're not going to like the results! Do I make myself clear!"

"I'm not going nowhere with you! Get off me!"

"Yo, I know you heard what she said!" Mike stated, while taking off his skates. "I advise you to let go of her arm before we have a serious problem on our hands."

Slim hesitated for a second, then he slung me to the ground and attacked Mike. They rolled around on the floor for a little bit, until Mike's strength kicked in. He was able to position himself on top of Slim, putting his left hand around his throat, while he used his right hand to deliver crushing blows to Slim's face. He hit him six good times before security came and put us out. They fought again in the parking lot, but this time Mike knocked him out cold. We all jumped in the cars we came in after security intervened again and went to go eat. When we got to the restaurant I was surprised at how humble Mike was after just beating Slim up. The only thing he was worried about was whether or not I was okay. That was one of the things I loved about him. He was always in my corner and I knew he had my best interest at heart.

    The following afternoon when Mike dropped me off at home, there was a letter waiting for me. I couldn't believe my eyes at the sight of whose name was on the envelope. It was from none other than my mother Karen. I dreaded reading the letter, but a part of me was curious to know what she had to say. Especially after all she had done to me. I took a deep breath and began to read.

Dear Keya,

I know that I'm probably the last person that you ever want to hear from, but I had to write you this letter. During the four years that I've been locked away, not a day has gone by that I haven't thought about you, your brothers and the damage I caused. That monster that you had to live with for all those years wasn't the same loving mother that would've died for you. I allowed myself to be weak mentally and emotionally Keya and it led me to indulging in drugs and alcohol. I am so sorry baby. Now that I'm clean and sober, I realize that the things I've done are inexcusable and on numerous occasions I have seriously contemplated killing myself. Because of me you're forever scarred and I pray that it doesn't affect you from finding all the happiness you truly deserve and having a loving family of your own. I really don't expect you to forgive me, but if there's anything that I can do for you, please don't hesitate to let me know. I'm due to be released soon, and frankly, without my children in my life to some degree, I'd rather be dead. I know that love's not supposed to hurt, but no matter how much pain I ever exposed you to, Keya I do love you and I'm willing to do anything to prove it. Take care of yourself and I want to congratulate you early on graduating from high School. I am so proud of you baby.

Love Always, Mom

I sat in a daze while I let her letter marinate. How could she have the nerve to send me a letter after all she put me through? Robin must've sensed that something was wrong because she sat down beside me and put her arms around me. I handed her the letter while still managing to stay in my daze. When she finished reading the letter she held me tighter.

"Why couldn't she just leave me alone. I hate her so much," I said through sobs.

"I know, I know," Robin responded, while rubbing my head and neck trying to comfort me.

We continued to talk for a while about my mom, relationships and something that always put a smile on my face; my beautiful niece Monteea. When I was stressed out about the whole Slim situation, she was the one that lifted my spirits up. I went downstairs with Robin and played with Monteea for a little before I went back upstairs. I sat on the edge of my bed for a second to collect my thoughts, then I grabbed a pen and paper.

Dear Karen,

You don't deserve the right for me to call you mom. Giving birth to a child doesn't necessarily make you a parent. As you can see, the responsibilities become even harder after that. You forgot the part where you were supposed to nurture me, protect me from all harm, and teach me all the finer points in life. Especially how to be a woman and how to conduct myself in a proper manner. Unlike you, my real mother instilled some great qualities in me. She taught me how to love, respect and have a sense of pride about myself. I love her unconditionally for taking me in and providing me with the same love as she did with her biological daughter. I'll never forgive you for making my life a living hell and knowing that you're suffering brings a sense of relief and peace within for me. I hope that I never see or hear from you again! My life is better without you Karen.

You're dead to me!

I was hesitant about sending the letter off at first, but she had to know how I felt about her, and the love I had for my new family. I wanted to go a little deeper and express how I truly felt, that I wished her and Frank were dead. I didn't go there because Momma Sue would never approve of me being disrespectful to any adults, even if it was the woman that pawned me off to support her drug and alcohol habits. I hoped the way that I did express myself would bring closure and she left me alone for good.

Two weeks later I received another letter from her. I couldn't believe the nerve of her to think we could continue corresponding with each other. How could she not acknowledge the permanent, internal scar that she helped put there? I thought about tossing the letter in the trash, but once again, I was overwhelmed by curiosity. I glanced at the envelope for several more seconds, and then I opened it.

Dear Keya,

I understand how you feel and I'm very sorry that I put you through those awful things. Your brothers have given me their forgiveness, but without all of my children, I told you that I'd rather be dead. Addiction is something some people never have the strength and willpower to overcome, but I had the opportunity to seek the help I needed and I did so. I can honestly say from a clean and sober standpoint that I love you with all my heart. Goodbye baby.

I was relieved that she finally got the message and had given up. In the days to come I didn't feel the same way. At an early age I learned that a person's thoughts became their actions. My mother definitely loved me and my brothers to death and she took her own life to prove her point. Guilt ran through my body as her last words were read at the funeral.

My journey on earth has reached its destination. Before I take my ride I just want my three beautiful children to know that no matter what we went through, I loved them with all my heart. I made some terrible decisions in my life and those costly mistakes destroyed our foundation. Inside I cried for help, but I didn't push myself enough to go get it. I did a whole lot of self-inventory during my incarceration and as I gradually started loving myself, I became a better person. Nothing in life mattered to me without the love and forgiveness of my children, so I decided

my time on earth was up. As my soul leaves my body, I pray that God will forgive me for my sins and open up the gates to Heaven for me. Keya, Eddie and Kenny, I love y'all so much.

Forever,

Mom

As I laid the flowers on her casket I shed a few tears. I closed my eyes and asked God for forgiveness. I had the power to save her life and I didn't make an effort to do so. There wasn't that much hatred in the world. Before I left I told her that I forgave her and that I loved her very much.

For the next couple of weeks I isolated myself from everybody and just sat around reminiscing about all the good times me and my mother shared. She used to sing to me while she did my hair and walked me to school. I realized that before the drugs and alcohol, she was a great mother. I silently prayed that the good outweighed the bad and that she went to Heaven. She at least deserved to rest in peace.

CHAPTER 4

Mike came home and spent quality time with me as much as he could, but our relationship didn't have that fire it once had. I don't know if I was starting to outgrow him or what. I just felt like there were other things that I wanted to do. When my mom took her own life it helped me realize how precious life is and I decided to insert something that Momma Sue told me years ago. She told me to dream as if I'll live forever and live as if I'll die today. I still loved the sex that Mike was putting on me, so I gave him an ultimatum he couldn't refuse. I gave him the option to mess with anybody he wanted to, but when I called he better come running.

"What part of the game is that!" He snapped. "Do you have somebody else you mess with?"

"No, it's not like that. When I get in my moods where I don't want to be bothered I don't want you to feel rejected."

"I don't agree with this so called arrangement you put together. If you want somebody else just say so."

"I told you that's not it baby."

"Yeah okay. Tell me anything."

"I swear to you! This is not about me wanting somebody else!"

"I hear you. I don't feel like arguing with you about this though."

"Thank you. Everything will work out just fine baby."

And things did work out just fine. He got the opportunity to have his cake and eat it without any repercussions or pressure on him. Plus my baby ran like a track star whenever I made that call. My sisters all told me that I was crazy for giving him so much breathing room, but it made things a lot less complicated for me. They're the ones that had to go through the stress of their men cheating. Me on the other hand, I was in total control. He never cheated on me because he knew I expected him to or let's just say he was very discreet if he did cheat. The reverse phycology tactic I used worked to perfection. But no matter how much I told myself that I was outgrowing my relationship with Mike, I didn't want to lose him.

Momma Sue and Mr. Damon felt like it was time for them to move on, so they packed up and moved to Charlotte. They asked me and Robin to come with them, but we both declined. Robin and Mont stayed at our house, while me and Janet got our own apartment. The apartment was built like two separate houses, which was good for our privacy. It was located in Oakland, a few blocks from the University of Pittsburgh. The location was perfect, since we were enrolled there. I used some of the money I took from Slim to buy me a Ford Taurus to get around in. It was a cute car, but the most important thing to me was that it was mines. It got me from A to Z with no problem, unlike the jealous tramps that constantly had their thumbs out waiting for a ride.

When it was actually time for me and Janet to start school, the first week or so was a drag for me. We finally got to know people and found out about the different fraternity parties and things that went down on campus. A girl that we met named Sarah invited us to her party. She was part of the cheerleading squad for the men's basketball team and we expressed our interest in trying out for the squad.

The weekend of the party finally came. I was a little nervous because everyone at the party would be total strangers to us and I didn't know what to expect. We began putting the finishing touches on our make-overs before we hit the road.

"Perfection," I said, as I looked at my beautiful reflection in the bathroom mirror.

"Do I aim to please Sis?" Janet asked me.

"As you always do," I responded.

On that note, the showstoppers hit the road. When we got to the address Sarah gave us, we could hear Snoop Dogg's, Gin and Juice playing from the parking lot. We took one last glance in the mirror, then headed towards the party. When we got inside everybody was on the dance floor except the dee-jay, the guy who served the beer from the keg and the person letting people in and out of the party. Me and Janet didn't drink, so we just walked around trying to find Sarah instead. It took us nearly fifteen minutes to track her down, but being that she was engaged in an intense kissing and grinding session, we kept it moving. Ten minutes later we bumped into her again. This time she wasn't lip locking.

"Are y'all having a good time so far?" She asked, with a forced smile.

"Not really. Everyone in here is a total stranger to us," I said, being straight up.

"Oh, that's not a problem. I can change that. Come on, follow me," She told us, holding me by the hand.

We walked through a maze of people and stopped by three tall and very attractive guys. One of the faces was familiar because he was the one Sarah was getting busy with when we came in.

"Jay and Tony, I want y'all to meet my friends Keya and Janet. They're freshman's here and I was just trying to get them acquainted with a few people. Can I count on y'all to be perfect gentleman?"

"You know they're in good hands with us," the guy named Tony told her.

"That's exactly why I brought them over here. I knew I could count on y'all."

After the formal greeting we held general conversations with Jay and Tony. Me and Tony exchanged pleasantries and I learned that he was a sophomore who played forward for the basketball team. He quickly threw it out there that he didn't have a girlfriend, which I told myself was a lie. It didn't matter anyway because I immediately informed him that I had a man. One of the things we had in common was majoring in Business Management. We continued to converse throughout the evening and he eventually asked me to dance. Tony was an excellent dancer and it surprised me how light he was on his feet. He had a lot of confidence in his dancing ability. We danced for three straight songs, but I had to stop when my feet started hurting me. We conversed a little longer until me and Janet began to get tired. They offered to take us out to eat before we went home, but we declined and headed towards the door.

"Keya, hold up for a second," Tony called out, walking towards us.

"What's up?" I asked.

"I forgot to give you my number."

"I can't accept your number. I told you that I have a boyfriend, remember."

"I don't mean it like that. I'm just trying to be your friend."

"Oh, okay. I apologize for assuming. We'll see each other around then friend. With all the girls on campus I'm sure you won't lose no sleep if we didn't."

"You have a real sense of humor," he said with a smile.

"Good night Tony. It was nice meeting you," I shared, before me and Janet got in my car and drove off.

For some strange reason we were both re-energized when we got home, so we decided to stay up and watch a movie. Ty gave Janet a bootleg copy of the movie Menace II Society, so we popped it in. We had us a big bowl of Cool Ranch Dorito's and lemonade as our refreshments and we both sat Indian-Style on our living room pillows. I fell asleep halfway into the movie, only waking up from Janet telling me to go to bed. The strangest thing happened to me when I went to my room and fell back to sleep. I had a dream that I had to choose who I wanted to be with. It was either Mike or Tony. When I found myself in Tony's arms I jumped up out my sleep. I looked around the dark room and realized that I was all alone. I glanced at the clock and it read 10:27am.
I made a mental note to change the curtains because they were so dark light could barely get through. When I got myself situated Janet was already up and moving around.

"I sure do miss my Ty Ty," she blurted out.

"Yeah, I know the feeling. I miss Mike too, but you know football's about to start and that's their priority right now," I explained.

"Well, he needs to hurry up home because I can't take being around all those fine men."

"I feel the same way, but we have to be strong. Last night, well this morning, I had a dream that I had to choose between Mike and Tony."

"Wow Key! And what did you do, or should I not ask a stupid question?"

"I don't remember giving any of them an answer, but I ended up in Tony's arms and that's when I woke up."

"I can't blame you for thinking about Tony. He is sexy. I wouldn't mind seeing what Jay was working with."

"Damn! What happened to I miss my Ty Ty?"

"We're one in the same Keya. You can love and miss someone and have fantasies about another person."

"I guess you're right Sis. So does that mean you're going to kick it with Jay?"

"Ain't nothing wrong with having a side piece. We both know that Ty has one."

"I tried to tell y'all that a long time ago, but I was the crazy one. I gave Mike freedom to venture out, but my intentions were never to mess with other people."

"That's understandable and I feel you one hundred percent. We both have to be mindful that there's so much to experience in life. I'm not just talking about messing with other guys either. This college thing can be a wonderful experience if we remember to stay open minded."

"I guess you're right."

We went to visit Kelly to spend a little time with our niece Keesha, then we stopped by Robin's to give Monteea that same love and affection. It appeared that me and Janet had a little too much energy for the princess, because she was sound asleep after only twenty minutes into our visit. We gossiped with Robin for another half hour, then we headed home.

I wanted to ride around through Oakland to see who was out, but Janet declined. She thought she needed a make-over. We had to ride pass the Original's to get home though. The Original's was a huge restaurant where most of the college students ate and hung out at. It was also an after hour spot when the clubs and bars closed. Anything you could think of eating they had it at the Original's.

As we were riding by we just so happened to see Tony and Jay walking towards a parking lot near the Original's. Janet pleaded with me not to pull over, but I couldn't resist.

"Hey friend," I hollered out the window to Tony.

"Hey back to you. I was wondering when I would see you again."

"I guess today is your lucky day," I flirted.

"I hope it is."

"I was speaking in regards to you visually seeing me. Any other thoughts you have need to be deleted."

"Thanks for putting me in my place."

"Well we were just passing through on our way home and we just happened to see y'all," Janet spoke.

"So does that mean you're telling me goodbye again?" Jay asked.

"It depends," Janet blurted out, not realizing what she just said.

"On what?" Jay continued to dig.

"If y'all can think of something else to do," she continued.

"We like to play spades," Tony joined in.

"And we're the best in spades," I said with confidence.

"Well follow us and it's on," Jay said.

It took ten minutes for us to get to their apartment. We both knew we were wrong, but we still went anyway. It was a cozy spot they had. Jay offered us something to drink, then we got started. We won the first three games, and they turned around and won the next four. We continued to go back and forth until Janet noticed that it was almost eleven in the evening.

"It's getting late fellas and I have to get ready for class tomorrow morning," Janet told them.

"So when will I see you again?" Jay asked her.

"Since I really enjoyed myself, I don't have a problem with doing this again soon."

"Do you speak for both of y'all?" Tony asked.

"I can speak for myself if you have something to ask me," I responded, walking towards the door.

"You got me a little gun shy. Last time you turned me down with no hesitation."

"I told you that I'm spoken for, but I don't see any harm in us being friends."

"What about friends with benefits?"

"I'm assuming you're talking about the benefits of having these card games."

"That wasn't exactly what I was talking about, but-."

"If you push too hard you might end up with nothing at all. Write your phone number down and we can talk on the phone from time to time."

"That's fair enough."

During the next few weeks we spent a lot of time playing cards and doing other things with Tony and Jay. When our calls began to decrease, Mike and Ty made it their business to come stay with us more. It felt good spending more time with my baby, but I couldn't stop thinking about Tony.

One evening we went to the movies with Tony and Jay. Things got pretty intense that night. It started off with a simple kiss, then we ended up at their apartment. Before me and Janet could take control of things, we were both having wild, passionate sex. The funny thing was, the sex was good as I imagined it to be. He must've thought I was a cold bitch though. As we laid side by side breathing hard, I told him that it couldn't happen again. I collected my things, went to get Janet, and we left.

On a daily basis, Janet constantly talked about how guilty she felt, but we knew what would eventually happen the first time we went to their apartment. I just blocked it out and pretended like it never happened. It was hard to do, especially when we ran into them every time we hung out with Sarah. I wanted to be true to Mike, but I wasn't getting enough sex, so we made arrangements with them to have sex once a week.

One night Janet had a late class, so I went to Tony's apartment on my own. When I entered the apartment all the lights were off. The T.V.s were the only thing that lit up the rooms. I didn't see Jay, so I assumed we were there all alone. Tony undressed me in the living room, then led me to the bedroom. This time it was different than our normal sexual encounters. He was much rougher, but I still liked it. He threw my legs on his shoulders and pounded my pussy like his life depended on it. Ooh it felt so good! In fact, it was feeling too good. I asked him to stop for a second to see if I was right. The condom had torn, and I asked him to put on another one. The last thing I needed was to get pregnant and it not be Mike's baby.

"I have to use the bathroom first, but I want you laying on your stomach when I get back."

Two minutes later he came back in the room and positioned himself behind me. When he penetrated me something was different. Either I was going crazy or his dick got bigger all of a sudden. I didn't say anything because it was feeling so good, but when he was finished I stopped him before he went to the bathroom again. I couldn't believe it when I saw Jay standing in front of me. I began to snap and curse out loud until Tony entered the room and

LOVE'S NOT SUPPOSED TO HURT

begged me to forgive them. They were afraid that I would cry rape. I just threatened that if they ever came near me again, I would call the police.

As much as I wanted to be mad at them for the stunt they pulled, I envied Janet because Jay was all that. I just happened to run into Jay after our incident when I stopped by the Original's. At the sight of me he started to take off, but I grabbed him by the arm.

"Me and you really need to sit down and talk," I told him.

"Listen Keya. I swear that wasn't my idea. I appreciate you not telling Janet about what happened too."

"I have my reasons and it can stay that way if you want."

"And what would it take for it to stay that way?"

"Come to my house and fuck me real good."

"What about Janet?"

"She's staying at her mom's house for the night, so I have the apartment all to myself."

"Let's go."

When we got to my apartment we never made it to my bedroom. Clothes went flying everywhere as we went straight at each other. Now that he didn't have to sneak the sex was even better. I wanted Jay so bad that I didn't even make him put on a condom. Damn it was so good. He sat me on the kitchen counter, spread my legs and drove deep inside of me. I tilted my head back, closed my eyes and savored the moment. I wanted to scream out his name with every thrust, but I elected to bite down on my lip instead. We were so into each other that we didn't hear Janet come in.

"Keya, I got a sur-."

The whole room went silent as she entered the apartment with Mike and Ty. From the look in Mike's eyes I thought me and Jay were dead. They all just shook their heads in disgust and left. How could I be so stupid to bring Jay to our house? We could've got a cheap hotel and now I'm in deep shit with my man and my sister.

I didn't want to be alone, so me and Jay went and got a hotel room. He held me all night without saying a word. In the morning he looked me in my eyes and gave me a long kiss.

"I'll always be here for you if you need me," he promised me.

"Thank you," I said, as I left the hotel to go to class.

Although nobody knew what happened except for the people that were there, I felt paranoid and I constantly looked from side to side and over my shoulders. I still had yet to run into Janet and I was confused about what I would say when I did see her. My last class came to an end, so I decided to head home. I figured it would be better if me and Janet crossed paths within the confines of our apartment. When I got there she was packing her things.

"I'm glad you're here," she told me. "If you were someone else we would be fighting like cats and dogs right now. I'm confused, hurt and I'm very disappointed in you Key. You knew I liked him and not only did you fuck him, you brought him to our apartment. So what were you planning to do, keep fucking him while I fucked him too? You, Kelly and Robin are my backbones, so imagine how it feels having you stab me in the back. I can't be around you right now and I don't know if I'll ever be able to. My share of the rent will continue to get paid until the lease is up, but I need time and space away from you."

As bad as I wanted to say something to her, to tell her that I was sorry, I respected her wishes and went to my room. I locked my door and tried to find something on T.V, but I could not find nothing of interest. I needed somebody to talk to, but since Momma Sue was now in Charlotte, I was forced to work things out on my own. I just need to vent, so I jumped in my car and drove to the cemetery. I got down on bended knees next to her tombstone and poured my heart out.

"Mom, what have I become? I always find a way to destroy anything good in my life. I do things to degrade myself, my family and anybody else that loves, care for and believes in me. I guess I'm taking all the wrong steps to find love or to be accepted. Could it be that I'm a reflection of you at your worst? Janet is so upset with me that she can't stand to even look at me and Mike walked in on me while I was having sex with Janet's male friend. I wish I knew a way to fix things, but I think it's beyond repair. I feel so empty inside right now and the best way for me to ease the pain might be to join you. Momma Sue is long gone and I don't have anyone else to turn to. Can you please help me make some sense of this? Out of all the times that you were never there for me, why couldn't you be here to come through for me now?"

I sat there in silence for a few minutes, and then I jumped in my car and took a long ride to nowhere in particular. I just wanted to finish clearing my head. My life was all screwed up and I had no idea where to start at to fix things. Robin and Kelly was an option, but I knew they wouldn't approve of my actions either. I betrayed our sisterhood by stabbing Janet in the back. Maybe some time alone in the apartment would help me find a resolution. I headed back home, praying that Janet was long gone so that the guilt didn't continue to cut through me like a sharp knife. There was no sign of her car, which was a huge relief. I walked inside my apartment and Janet's presence was already missed. Although the only thing she took were her clothes and other personal items, the house felt vacant like when we first moved in. The more I looked around the room, the more the guilt continued to kick in. I started hyperventilating, so I ran to the kitchen and tried as best I could to drink some water. After a few deep breaths I felt a little better, but there was something I had to do to clear my conscience. I picked up the phone to call Momma Sue and told her about everything that happened. Even the visit to my mother's grave. She was silent for a moment I guess to get her thoughts together before she decided to speak.

"For starters, how do you think that made you look sleeping with a man your roommate was involved with? Don't even answer, just listen. I understand that you've experienced traumatic situations as a child, but you need to figure out if you're going to keep using that, and Karen as an excuse. Or you have a choice to conduct yourself in a way I know you're capable of. The decisions we make pretty much define who we are and what we'll become. You're not a whore or slut Keya, but if you constantly conduct yourself in that type of manner, how could I beg to differ? I don't know how long it will take, Janet will come around eventually. The relationship y'all shared will probably never be the same, but she loves you too much to never speak to you again. My invitation is still there for you to come live with us. Besides that, I can't be there to guide and protect you. I'll always be your voice of reasoning, but you have to make better decisions. I love you and we'll talk again later."

As I sat back and digested everything Momma Sue said to me, I cried all night wishing I could take back all the bad I've done, I knew that I would have to face my sister sooner or later, I just needed more time to get myself together first.

The next few weeks that passed by, I went to my classes and came straight home. I ran into Jay and I told him that it wouldn't be a good idea for us to see each other anymore. Before he could respond, I walked away. The only person that I had any communication with was my next door neighbor, and even that was to a minimum. I rented movies from Block Buster, and kept to myself. I was really beginning to find a sense of peace too.

One night when I was finishing up my work for one of my exams I had coming up, I heard a knock at my door. At first I didn't answer it, because I was used to Janet getting the door when someone came by. I kept hearing soft knocks and it dawned on me that I was all alone. I threw on my robe to go see who it was. I assumed it was my neighbor, but it was one o'clock in the morning.

"Who is it?" I hollered, as I walked through the living room to answer the door.

For some strange reason I thought I heard the male voice say Mike, and I unlocked the door without double checking. Two guys dressed in all black, with masks on, rushed through my door. Before I was able to scream, one of them grabbed me by the throat, while the other one shut the door and locked it. The one guy continued to choke me, while the other one grabbed my legs as they carried me to the bedroom. I kept trying to make out the voices, but they spoke in whispers. Once we got to my bedroom, they slammed me roughly on the bed.

"Please don't do this to me!" I pleaded.

The guy that was choking me slapped me so hard across my face that I briefly lost my hearing.

"Bitch, if you try to scream, I swear I'll kill you," he said through clenched teeth.

He showed me a gun to let me know he was serious, then they ripped off my clothes and roughly turned me on my stomach. I felt a couple of fingers go in and out of me. He did that for a minute before he went to my anal area. It felt like a thumb shoved in my ass, but he pulled it right out. A second later I heard the faint sound of a zipper being pulled down; a sign that one of them were taking their pants off. He slammed his dick inside me and pumped like a mad man. Though it felt like he intended to rip my insides out, I did everything in my power to keep from screaming. My life depended on it. I tried to fight and wiggle my way out of his grasp when he attempted to put it in my ass. That bright idea came to a complete halt when he hit me so hard in my ribs that I could hardly breathe. They both pretty much beat me into submission. Once again, he pumped like a mad man.

It was the worse pain that I ever felt in my life. I had to bite on my blanket to keep from yelling.

When the torture was over, the guy made me get on my knees and face him. The slightest movement made the pain even greater. After pulling his pants down, he ordered me to suck his dick. My eyes were burning from all the tears I shed, but I managed to see a scar on his left thigh. As he stuffed his dick into my mouth I bit down on it as hard as I could. It was also the last thing that I remember doing.

My neighbor apparently called the police and told them that she heard a man screaming from the apartment next door. When her boyfriend peaked out the door to see what was going on, he noticed that my apartment door was wide open. He found me lying unconscious on the floor, and immediately called the ambulance. Miraculously I survived. Nevertheless, I wish they would've just left me for dead. I suffered a concussion, along with a broken nose. My eyes were so swollen that I couldn't see. They were sealed shut. My jaw was broke and I had broken ribs. I also had a busted up rectum. I could hear people in my hospital room there to support me, but the wires around my jaw prevented me from talking. I had to wait almost two weeks for the swelling on my eyes to go down so I could see. When my sight re-emerged, Robin, Kelly, my two brothers, Uncle Greg and even Janet were there. Momma Sue and Mr. Damon found time to fly in and support me too. Despite having my support team by my side, thoughts of the horrible event had me terrified. Every single time that I moved the pain that shot through me brought back images of Frank and the other two men that violated me. I wish my neighbors would've just let me die.

The detectives constantly came by to talk to me, but I didn't have any intentions on confiding in them, because they had already failed me once. I didn't see why I should set myself up for failure again. I also had a surprise visit from Mike. There was so much that I needed to say to him. I was frustrated because all I could do was listen to what he had to say, being that my mouth was still wired up.

"Hey Key," he said in a whisper. "It's good to see that you're doing better. Kelly told me that you were cool, but I had to come see for myself. I had plans on coming by much sooner. I've been struggling in school lately, so I had to address that issue. Everything has changed in my life since that day. I thought about killing myself, killing you and quitting football. At the end of the day you practically warned me when you gave me permission to be with other girls. I should've argued with you until that ridiculous idea left your thoughts. I wasn't in agreement with that, because everything that I wanted in life was you. Keya, I have never loved anyone the way I love you. I love you more than I love myself. That might sound crazy, but it's real. I've been searching for every reason in the world to forgive you, but love's not enough to ignore the images that I have of you and him. I don't totally blame you, because had I not been cheating, you wouldn't have had so much free time on your hands. I just wish I knew who did this to you so I can get all my frustration out."

I reached for his hand as tears began to roll down my cheeks. He placed my hand in his, then raised it to his lips to kiss it.

"If I ever find out who did this to you their asses is mines."

The law had failed me, but Mike always had my best interest. I pointed next to the tablet and pen that was sitting next to my bed. Mike grabbed it and handed it to me. I took a deep breath and wrote down, "it was Slim." I continued writing and told him I knew it was Slim because of the scar on his thigh. I then dropped the pen down and started crying uncontrollably. He held me tight and promised me that it would be okay.

"Robin told me about what happened to you when you were younger, so this is even more personal for me."

When Robin came to see me the next day, she told me about my Uncle Greg, Mike, Mont and Ty. They were looking for Slim day and night, with plans on killing him. I couldn't stand to see any of them go to jail, so I asked Robin to contact the detectives for me. I provided them with all the information they needed. I just prayed that they tracked Slim down before Mike and the others did.

Mike came to check on me every day and I tried my best to keep him there with me. It was a lost cause, he was determined to find Slim. My prayers were answered when the detectives came to the hospital a few days later. They informed me that Slim was taken into custody. They also told me that his penis was still badly bruised, from when I told them I tried to bite it off. I came to learn that Slim was really a pussycat. The heroin that he put in his system made him feel like he was a thug. He was only locked up for three days before he started spilling his guts.

I felt much safer knowing Slim and his accomplice would be locked away until trial. With that being said, good news usually came in packs. A friend of my Uncle, who's serving life in prison, killed someone connected to my past. The hard criminals have a no mercy rule on child molesters and rapists. Word got out that Frank raped Greg Gibson's niece and he was killed a few months before his release. Trapper the guy that ended Frank's life, knew of what Frank had done from day one. He just wanted to torment and extort Frank until he got close to his release date.

I was finally released from the hospital and Robin ordered me to stay with her and Ty until I got well. I planned to move to Charlotte with Momma Sue and Mr. Damon. Although all the people that caused me harm were either dead or in jail, I was still afraid.

I went grocery shopping with Robin one day and it was jam packed. I ran into a few people that I knew and they made me feel comfortable with the kind words they spoke. When we were on our way to get in line to pay for our food, I heard someone shout my name. He verbally assaulted me, calling me a variety of degrading names.

"And you had the nerve to turn your nose up at me. Two people fucked you at the same time! Bitch, you got exactly what you deserved!"

Rodney still had a grudge against me from the time I turned him down in high school. My self-esteem was already low, but after he humiliated me in front of all those people, I had none left. I ran out the store crying and waited for Robin to come out. She tried to comfort me, but I just wanted to hurry home.

When we arrived at the house, I contemplated different ways to take my own life. I felt like an outcast, worthless; like I didn't belong. I ran upstairs to the bathroom so I could follow through with the plan I came up with. I searched for a razor and when I couldn't find one, I broke a glass that was on the sink. I immediately started cutting away at my wrist.

"Keya are you okay?" Robin shouted to me after she heard the glass break. "KEYA!" She began screaming while she pounded on the door. "Ty, see if you can get in there!" She told him, in a panicked voice.

He kicked in the door and they found me lying on the floor with both of my wrist bleeding. Ty picked me up and they rushed me to the hospital. Much to my distaste, I managed to avoid death again. The doctors had me under very close observation, which prevented me from finishing the job. No matter who came to visit me, I refused to talk. I didn't eat and I didn't bathe. Everybody thought I was going crazy, so Momma Sue and Uncle Greg made a difficult decision and checked me into a mental institution. If they thought I was crazy before, it really messed everybody up when I completely flipped out. I was eventually confined in a strait jacket. The once beautiful, young diva, now looked like a deranged lunatic. I had to see a therapist twice a day, who I gave a hard time by simply ignoring her. I also ignored everyone else, because I just wanted to be left alone to die. What made me rekindle my sanity, was the surprise visit from Melissa, our cheerleading captain in high school.

"Hello Keya, I'm sorry about all the pain you've endured. A long time ago when I gave y'all a few pieces of advice, I left a few things out. The reason was because I prayed this speech would never be needed. I was raped when I was fourteen, by my boyfriend at the time. It was the most traumatic, horrific experience in my life.

"How did you overcome that feeling?" I asked, speaking my first words in weeks.

"Counseling and the support of my family and friends. We all handle situations differently though. You have to want help in order to receive it. If you want, I'll be here every step of the way to help you overcome this."

"You're so mentally strong. I don't know if I'll ever be able to reach that point."

"Keya, you have to fight for what you want and believe in."

"Melissa, I don't know what I did to deserve this!" I said, breaking down in tears. "I just want to get better! I want to be my old self again!"

"It's okay," she said, holding me tight. "We're going to make you better than your old self."

I stopped being rebellious towards the staff and all the other people that were supportive of me. I thought that was important for me to do in order to have a fighting chance against the demons I have inside of me. My psychiatrist came to see me twice a day like she normally did, and the healing process began. We started off by me telling her how I felt mentally, emotionally and physically. Upon my request, Melissa sat in on our sessions three times a week and it really helped me open up. I told her that everything was perfect for me growing up, until the day my father put his hands on my mother.

"Did you ever witness any of the beatings taking place?"

"Yes," I told her. "It was only that one time. Then he started staying out late or not coming home at all. When my father went to jail, my mom was in and out of abusive relationships. My brother Eddie's father use to hit her for no reason. One time he threw her down a flight of stairs while she was pregnant. She finally built up the courage to leave him. The only problem was that she substituted the men with drugs and alcohol."

"Okay, that's enough for today. We'll resume again tomorrow. In the meantime, is there anything you need or anyone you would like to talk to?"

"Yes there is. I would like to make a phone call to my sister Janet."

"That's fine. I'll make arrangements for you to get a phone call immediately."

"Thank you so much."

I made the call about twenty minutes later, but the answering machine came on. I left a message for her to call me back as soon as she could. Three hours later she returned my call.

"Hey you," she said, sounding happy to hear from me.

"Hey you too."

"Everybody was just talking about you. We were worried because none of us heard from you."

"I know, and I want to apologize for that and everything else."

"You don't have to apologize."

"Yes I do, and please, just hear me out. I've done so much, and I've been through so much. I just wanted to die and avoid the pain; to prevent from causing anyone else more pain. I made a whole lot of irrational decisions that I wish I could take back. I never meant to hurt you. It was this demon inside me that manipulated my thoughts and actions. It might be a little too confusing for you to really understand though. The bottom line is that I'm fucked up in the head and I've been this way for a long time. I did everything that I could think of to avoid being lonely, because my horrible childhood always resurfaced."

"Keya believe me, I do understand. Had I known all of this before, we could've took a different approach on a lot of things. I want to share something with you that my mother shared with me when I ran into a dead end in my life. She told me that, what was, is not, and never again will be. That's a true statement only if you believe. It's important for us to be cautious of the things we think about, because a lot of our thoughts become actions. I think you're going to be better than ever. I love you Sis."

"I love you too."

I desperately wanted to get better so I could get back home to the people that loved me. First I had to learn how to love myself. Melissa and my shrink warned me about trying to look too far ahead though.

In order for me to properly heal, the process would be like taking baby steps, one day at a time.

I was doing so well in my individual sessions, that I was told to get ready for the next phase. The next phase consisted of a group sessions. It felt awkward to me, so I just sat there and listened. I always felt inside like I was the only person who experienced the type of trauma I have, but a lot of the women who spoke went through some horrible events.

"My name is Maxine and I was married for nine long years. I was a victim of domestic violence for seven of those years. The first two years were the best and happiest moments of my life, but that loving husband turned into a monster. He began beating me for the smallest things. Like, there was a time when I had my daughter and he broke my arm because I still had the baby fat on me eight months later. There were so many different encounters that it would take a lifetime to give dialogue. To make a long story short; during the course of those seven years' worth of beatings, I suffered a cracked cranium, broken arms and legs, fractured ribs and many more terrible injuries. My brother couldn't take it any longer and he killed Simon. Now he's doing fifteen to thirty years in prison because I was too weak and afraid to leave my husband."

"Hi everybody, my name is Dorothy. My stepfather raped me on three separate occasions. When I finally got the nerve to stand up to him, he beat me, and then set the house on fire while I was still in it. Lucky for me, the neighbor came and rescued me before there was any real damage done. I had minor burns, which have since healed. When I told my mother the truth about what happened, she called me every insulting name she could think of. When the lab results came back from the semen that was found inside of me, he was prosecuted for arson and rape. I never spoke to my mother again. Up until recently, I haven't been able to cope with my situation."

"Hello everyone, I'm Jessica. I was also a victim of rape. Being that I'm the only child, my Uncle Marcus used to give me the world and take me everywhere. His wife also loved me to death. They separated when I was in my freshman year of high school. There were days that I stayed over his house and went to school from there. My mom didn't like me staying at home alone when she worked late. During those times, my uncle would walk in the bathroom and try to help wash me up while I was in the bathtub. That turned into him fondling me and he eventually began performing sexual acts on me. He would make me give him oral sex and fuck me in the ass. We never had sex the conventional way. I was terrified of him. I didn't have anyone to turn to because my uncle was always the one that protected me from everything. I stopped going to his house and avoided him when he came to mines. The times that I couldn't avoid him, I would shake uncontrollably with fear. My mom would always ask me what was wrong, but I was too afraid to tell her. One day, when I came home from school, my uncle was there waiting on me. He snatched me up aggressively and led me to my bedroom. As soon as we entered, he ripped off my clothes and made me lay on my stomach. He forced himself in my ass and I screamed my lungs out. My mom ran through the door and she was horrified by what she saw. She ran to get her gun, but he managed to escape. He eventually got apprehended. When I had to testify and re-live those horrible moments, I ended up here."

I didn't speak until a few days later. But just being in that environment with a group of ladies that went through similar situations and struggles as me was very therapeutic to me. After four months of intense counseling, I was committed to outpatient therapy.

CHAPTER 5

    I wasn't totally comfortable with being home yet, after being in the hospital so long. I had grown accustomed to and found my comfort zone amongst the women who had gone through tragedies like I had. Although we all came from different walks of life, in some form or fashion, we were all one in the same. To be with them fighting for my pride, security and self-esteem, made all the sense in the world to me. I tried to protest to the staff about staying, but they assured me that it was time to move on. My last few days with them, I prayed that we all got through our ordeals, and find the love, peace and happiness that we deserved. I prayed extra hard for Jessica, because she was so young and innocent. Plus I could relate to her more being that we were around the same age when we were raped. Looking back at everything now, it would've been a good idea for me to seek professional help back then. All the love and affection that I received altered that decision. Jessica's recovery will probably be much tougher because of what her uncle meant to her. For the most part he was her rock; someone that she loved, looked up to and called upon for anything. The great thing that she had going for her, was the excellent staff members she had to help her out. On top of that, I gave her my word that I would always stay in touch.

    Although I wasn't in my comfort zone, it felt good to be surrounded by family, friends and loved one's. Momma Sue and Mr. Damon even came back to Pittsburgh to stay with me for a few weeks. It was a blessing having her there, she was my rock. Since the very first day that I moved in with her and Robin, Momma Sue was always like a security blanket for me.

Ty was still in school playing football. He came home as much as he could, but sometimes he would be gone for weeks at a time during football season. So quite naturally, having me back home meant the world to Robin. My bundle of joy was also happy to see Auntie back. If there was one person that could breathe life back into me, it was Monteea.

Melissa continued being very supportive to me as well. She stopped by the house on a regular basis, and she also attended all my outpatient sessions with me. Melissa was a remarkable friend.

Kelly brought Keesha by to see me a few times a week. She was so beautiful and precious. Little Ms. Busy Body was the other person that could breathe life into me. Kelly also delivered flowers and sweet messages to me from Mike. After all I put him through, his love still ran deep for me, which I truly cherished.

Surprisingly, my relationship with Janet had gotten stronger than it ever was. To assure that it never diminished again, we made a personal pledge to always love, trust and respect each other.

My Uncle Greg came to see me when he could. My brothers were running him around like crazy, going in and out of juvenile detention.

On my birthday, Momma Sue, Robin, Janet, Kelly and Melissa took me to get pampered. The massage really helped me release a lot of tension that I had built up inside of me. The sounds of birds chirping and heavy waters splashing took me to a peaceful place; one that I could've stayed at forever. When the massage therapist told me that we were done, I was so disappointed that I started to pay for another session. I didn't think things would turn out as well as they did, especially after the shaky start when I first entered the salon. Originally, a masseur was supposed to service me, but I refused to even go in the same room with him. We were all enjoying ourselves so much, that nobody thought about the mental affect it would have on me, having a male do my massage. After I flipped out a little bit, I was sent to a room where there was a masseuse at.

The rest of my day was even better. I had a hair appointment at La-La's, the best hair stylist in town. During my three hour make-over, I got a manicure and a pedicure. I couldn't believe the end results. Not only did I feel great, I actually looked like my old self again. We hit the mall afterwards, and then they took me out to eat later that evening. I had a great time, and we even ran into a few of the girls that were on the cheerleading squad with us. Together, we all laughed the night away. I believe Melissa had a lot to do with all of us being together like that. It was so like her to do something of that nature. She would always preach to us that we were our own sorority, no matter what directions we took in life. On this particular day, my birthday; it felt like it too, and we all promised to keep in touch more. As promised, we communicated with each other more, and instead of continuing to isolate myself by staying locked up in the house like a prisoner, I began to gradually go outside. My discomfort of being around men slowly began to fade away, mainly because I was never alone.

Me and my sisters went to the movies one evening, and then I let them talk me into going to the club afterwards. We danced amongst each other until this guy walked up to me.

"I see you and your friends are having a good time. I apologize for interfering with that, but I couldn't resist asking you to dance."

"No thank you," I told him.

"Are you sure? I'm an excellent dancer."

"I'm positive," I said quickly, but trying not to sound cruel.

"Well can I at least buy you a drink?"

"I don't drink."

"Damn, you definitely know how to give a guy the cold shoulder. You make me feel like I did something wrong to you. I'm afraid of your reaction if I asked you what your name was."

"How about not asking then," I said, with irritation in my voice.

"You know what Ms. Lady. I just want to apologize for whoever made you this angry."

He chuckled under his breath, shook his head, then walked away. Instead of rejoining my sisters who started dancing again when he walked away, I kept my eyes on him until he disappeared in the crowd. When the club was letting out, we ran into him again.

"I really hope you enjoyed yourself," he told me.

"Thanks to my sisters, I had a great time," I responded in a smart tone.

"Well I'm happy for you. Have a good night beautiful," he told me, ignoring my tone.

When I got home, I thought about all the fun I had and the situation I had with the guy. I knew that I didn't have to be that harsh, because all men weren't the same, but at that very moment, that was the only defense mechanism that I had. I sat down with Robin, and asked her what she thought about my actions.

"Honestly Sis, I thought it was about to be much worse than it actually was. When he wouldn't go away, I was prepared for you to snap. Thank God you didn't."

"I wouldn't have gone that far. He wasn't disrespectful or anything like that."

"Sis everybody's not a monster and I believe you know that. You'll be okay though, I got your back."

"I know you do. You always have. That's why I love you so much."

I continued to go outside, but never alone, and no more clubs. I didn't want to leave myself vulnerable to where guys could freely walk up on me. Instead, I spent most of my time at Bible Study or Church with Melissa and her mother. It was a little awkward for me at first, until I kept hearing things I could relate to. There was one thing in particular the pastor said that really hit home. He said that in order to reach your destination, you had to embrace your journey, and that God never puts us in situations we can't handle. He also recited Romans 12:2, which made me think. Romans 12:2 says; and do not be conformed to this world, but be transformed by the renewing of your mind, so that you may prove what the will of God is, that which is good and acceptable and perfect.

The problem for me, was that I didn't have a destination. I just existed . I was in college and what not, but I didn't have any goals and dreams outside of being on the cheerleading squad. In all reality, I think anything that could've helped me forget my childhood was a goal. I didn't quite understand why I had to go through the horrible experiences that I did, and now that I had done so, what would my reward be? I prayed to God every night and asked him the same things, but the answers never came. Instead of allowing myself to stay frustrated, I decided to start living and stop existing. I set some realistic short term goals that consisted of me finishing school, and putting the rest of my horrible past behind me. Before that could happen, there was something that I had to do. I contacted a few people and got Slim's address. I fought with myself about whether or not I should write him, then I started venting.

Slim,

First of all, this is not a friendly or love letter. I just have a few things that I need to get off my chest. I don't know if it was the drugs you were using, or if you always abused and tortured women. I hope the fifteen years in prison was worth it. I pray that your mother, or any other female in your family doesn't have to go through what you put me through. I don't know what you set out to accomplish, you sick son of a bitch! Even if it takes the entire fifteen years for you to digest this, here's a news flash for you! I may have been temporarily humiliated, but this bitch, as you casually called me, came out of that ordeal

stronger than ever! The joke is on you bastard, I got the last laugh! I hope you fight them guys in there like you fought me, because somebody might want a piece of your ass! Oh and one last thing. Make sure you keep your soap on the rope bitch!!!

I typed the letter and put a fake return address on the envelope. My uncle told me that he had a big surprise for Slim, so I wanted him to receive a few harsh words before that surprise reached him. Uncle Greg was the only person who knew about the letter I wrote. I didn't want to hear all the lectures from everyone else. Plus, that's what I needed to do in order to have closure on my past. I felt relieved that I was finally able to close that chapter of my life.

When I started back to school, everything was the exact same. The only difference was that everyone moved up a year, and I lived at home instead of that apartment. I even ran into Jay and Tony on separate occasions, and they were very polite to me. I also ran into Sarah, who quickly invited me to a party she was throwing, and I turned her down even quicker.

A guy approached me one day when I was leaving my last class. There were a lot of people around, so I felt safe for the time being.

"Excuse me, is your name Keya?" He asked me.

"Who wants to know?"

"My name is Prince. I'm Slim's cousin."

"And what can I do for you Prince?"

"It ain't what you can do for me. It's what I'm going to do to you bitch, if you don't go to the D.A. and tell them you lied."

I wanted to laugh in the one hundred and twenty pound nerds face, but I walked off acting scared so he could follow me. As soon as I got near my car I turned around and sprayed him with mace, then I kicked him in the balls. He was hollering and screaming like the bitch he called me. I drove straight to my Uncle Greg's house. When I told him what happened, he was pissed.

"You're not going back to that school! I knew I should've stopped you when you mentioned going back!"

I wanted to take his advice, but I had goals to reach. I didn't want to leave any stones unturned and not accomplish all my short term goals. We went back and forth about it, until he finally gave in.

"I'm taking you to and from school until I can get Slim's surprise together."

"I have no objections to that," I told him.

Him taking me to school only lasted three weeks. He was buying time until Trapper got his hands on Slim. He approached Slim with three other guys that were booty bandits, and let them have their way with Slim. No longer was he this tough, arrogant guy that loved to abuse women. He was now somebody else's bitch. My uncle told me stories about how Slim was using cool-aid for lipstick, and the beatings he took when he wasn't where he was supposed to be. I thought he was exaggerating, until I saw the pictures to prove it. Slim was also ordered to call off the dogs, so I was cool to go to school without my uncle. I felt much more confident and secure now, and it showed in my body language. I was becoming my old self again. I just had to be cautious about making terrible mistakes like I did in the past.

Mike and his boys had finally graduated from college, but he was the only one that got drafted to the NFL. He was selected in the fourth round by the St. Louis Rams. It was an exciting time for everyone, including me, even though he was engaged to someone else, I didn't have a problem with that, and I told Mike how I felt. As much as I loved him and would always love him, the last thing that I needed was a man, because I was too busy learning to love myself. If he felt that she could do a good job making him happy, then I was happy for him. Mike's first pre-season game was being televised nationally against the Cincinnati Bengals, but everybody decided to go to the game and show our support. For me it was weird, because it was my first time watching him play since high school. He entered the game in the second quarter, and we were all excited.

He looked good wearing his favorite no. 2 jersey. From what I saw, it seemed like the game was a little too fast for Mike. His passes were thrown behind the receivers or too far over their heads. On one play he was almost tackled by a big lineman, but he managed to get away. As he was turning up the field, he was tackled from behind. He fell awkwardly to the ground, and we knew instantly that he was hurt. The medical team ran out on the field to tend to Mike, while we stood in the stands in disbelief. I threw my head in my lap and prayed that he would be okay. Ten minutes later he was taken off the field on a stretcher. It took a little time, but his parents found out what hospital he was taken to and we all rushed to where he was. They made us sit in the waiting room for two hours before anyone was allowed to see him. When his immediate family that included his mother, father, Kelly and his fiancée were the only ones permitted to see him, I was hurt. I deserved to be in there with him. I was a part of him that would always be there and I knew he'd want to see me.

I stayed calm and just waited to hear something. Forty-five minutes later, we found out that he had a torn ACL. I didn't know how serious it was, I just knew it was serious.

"He wants to see you," his mother told me.

We got on the elevator and rode up to the seventh floor. She then led me around a few corners where his room was at, and left us alone.

"Hey you," I said, not really knowing what else to say.

"What's up Key," he responded, obviously in pain.

"Your mom told me that you wanted to see me."

"Yeah I did tell her that. This is a time for me to be strong, and I needed someone to draw strength from."

"Wow, I feel so lucky."

He moved around a little bit grimacing, so I got up out my chair to help him. When I grabbed his arm, we both stopped and locked eyes.

"Your touch always felt so good," he told me.

"I don't think your future wife would approve of this."

"What, this?"

He pressed his lips against mines and gently put his hands on both of my cheeks. After a few pecks, I pulled away.

"She loves you Mike. We can't do this."

"Is this about you or her? I know what's inside my heart, and I'm just following it. I've been fighting these demons inside of me for a long time Keya, and now I'm finally ready to get it out my system. When I came to your apartment that day it killed me. Not only did it destroy me mentally and emotionally, my confidence as a football player was shattered. I've been playing on talent alone. My love for the game died when I lost you. I wanted to reach out to you a long time ago to let you know that I still loved you, but my pride wouldn't let me. I was too busy worrying about what people would think, and what it would do to my image, instead of just following my heart. Without you in it Keya, my life is incomplete."

"Wow, I really don't know what to say Mike. I'm sure you know that I'll always love you. You're the only man that I ever loved. I've been through a whole lot, and I can't just act off emotions. We have to be honest with each other. It's not as easy as it was when we were younger. There are other people's feelings involved. You made a commitment to spend the rest of your life with her. The same way you just expressed how you felt mentally and emotionally, think about her. What if you just up and leaving her causes her to do something to harm herself. Would you be able to live with yourself? I know you love me, and I love you too, but you can't turn people's feelings, or your feelings on and off like a light switch. Face her like a man and deal with your situation the way it's supposed to be handled. Don't cheat yourself out of life because of your love for me. I'm a different person Mike, and I'm finally getting the hang of loving myself."

"So basically, you're telling me to fuck off."

"I would never tell you that. You just need to take your time and think about what you really want. That evaluation has to be done without you quickly acting off your emotions. So like I said, take some time and think about this and we'll talk about it later. Is that fair?"

"Yeah that's fair," he agreed.

In the months to come, he moved back to Pittsburgh so he could start his rehab. Because of where he was selected at, Mike's contract wasn't guaranteed, so him getting healthy meant everything. I thought a lot about going to see him, to see how he was doing, but I didn't want to complicate things any further with his relationship. When I got a call from Sheila, I thought something had happened to Mike. Why else would she be calling me? Come to find out, she wanted to meet for lunch, and I agreed. I had to admit it; Mike had excellent taste in women. Sheila was beautiful in every way. She greeted me with a warm smile as we sat down.

"I called off the engagement," were the first words that came out her mouth.

"Why?" I asked, in total shock.

"Because, I'm not the one that he truly loves. I mean, he loves me in some ways, but what he feels for you is unconditional, undying love. Whenever your name comes up, he has this look in his eyes that's unexplainable. Keya, y'all belong together and as much as I love Mike, I won't stand in the way of that. Just promise me you'll make him happy. He deserves it."

"I won't sit here and deny how I feel about Mike. I will always love him, but I gave him my sincere blessing in regard to your engagement to him. Being in a relationship is the furthest thing from my mind right now."

"I understand Keya, believe me I do. I also know about the terrible tragedy you went through, and my heart goes out to you with hopes that the rest of your days will be filled with joy. We're not talking about a relationship here, it's your life. Besides, he needs you more than ever now. My flight leaves at three and I have no plans of coming back."

There was nothing I could say to Sheila, she already had her mind made up. When our brief lunch meeting was over, I went home and told Robin about everything that happened. I also asked her for her honest opinion.

"Truthfully, it doesn't matter what I think Sis. It's all about what your heart says."

"You know what my heart is saying."

"Well if you think sharing a life with Mike is the best thing for you, why fight it? I saw the look on your face when Sheila went in Mike's hospital room to see him with his parents. Do you want to risk being in the background again? If not, go get what's yours."

She didn't let me get a word in. When she finished expressing herself, she walked off. I had more questions to ask but in all reality, the answers were already there. I waited for a few days so I could process everything, then I went to go see Mike.

Kelly had called to tell me that he was struggling with his rehabilitation, and that seeing me might help. I never seen Mike look so vulnerable as he was in the hospital and the last thing I wanted was for things to get worse. I went to see him with the intent to talk some sense into him.

"Hey handsome," I called out when I entered the gym, where he was sitting on a bench. "Aren't you supposed to be pumping them muscles up?"

"What's up Key," he said dryly, totally ignoring my question.

"How have you been? It's seems like forever since the last time I saw you."

"To be exact, I was in the hospital in Cincinnati. It was the game that I got hurt."

"I wanted to reach out to you much sooner, but I didn't want to offend Sheila in any way."

"Sheila's long gone. What do you want Keya?"

"I want you to stop acting like an asshole Mike! Stop trying to be hard like nothing's bothering you, and that you don't need anybody! I know when you're hurting Mike, because I can feel it in my soul! Sheila told me that she broke off the engagement," I said, 'nearly-whispering. "Right now we need each other, to get through the pain we're both dealing with. If I'm wrong, all you have to do is say the word and I'll walk away."

"You think everything is that easy huh? Life is not as simple as you try to make it! When you're at odds with yourself mentally and emotionally, it's like the point of no return!"

"Baby I know, I know it's not easy. I've been there, and any obstacle can be overcome," I shared, still talking in a low voice. "The thing is, we have to start somewhere baby."

"It's too late. My career is over. I don't have anything left in my tank."

"Do you trust me Mike?"

"Of course I do, why would you ask me that?"

"Let's go get something to eat, and chill out for the day. Then we can start fresh in the morning working on your career."

"I don't know what I'll ever do without you."

"I'll always be here. From here on out, the only thing that can separate us is death."

We went to get a bite to eat, and then I spent the rest of the day talking to him while I laid in his arms. As I relaxed and just listened to his heartbeat, I knew I was where I was supposed to be. I had weathered the storm and embraced my journey, and now I had finally reached my destination.

Mike's rehabilitation process was slow, mainly because of his lack of enthusiasm. He didn't mind doing the easy part, getting himself together to go to the gym. When the physical, mental and emotional grind kicked in together; he would quit without a fight. I could understand it happening once or twice, but quitting became part of his daily routine. As much as I loved Mike, I couldn't afford to endure the stress that was coming my way at a rapid pace. The last thing I needed to do was back track and end up going nuts again. When I sat him down and told him how I felt, he basically brushed me off. I couldn't take it no more. He made me so mad that I had to let him have it.

"Mike, what the hell is wrong with you? How did you become so weak? The man that I knew and love was always strong and confident! Who are you? Where did Mike go?"

"What the fuck do you want from me? I told you when I lost my confidence!"

"Now we're getting somewhere. I'm the problem. If I wasn't around, would that make things better for you? The last thing I want to do is stop you from moving forward, so you can pursue your career."

"You know that I love you and I need you. It's just been hard for me to get motivated."

"Listen baby, I'm not good at throwing pity parties. Who would attend such a miserable event anyway? The last time I tried, I attempted suicide. Is that where you are in life? I've been through hell and back baby. The love and support that I got from you and everyone else really helped me kill the demons inside me. I should've confided in you about my past, but I didn't want to risk ever losing you. I didn't know how you would react, or if you would look at me totally different. When I cheated, it wasn't because I didn't love you anymore or because I liked him. I've been through some horrible experiences, and loneliness always brought back those dreadful memories. I never intended to hurt you, and I hope you believe me. Baby I am so thankful that you've forgiven me, and I'll never do anything to violate the love and trust that you have for me again. When I was in the hospital, there were women in there that went through tougher times than me. It gave me a whole new perspective on life, and to still be in position to live out my dreams, with the man of my dreams; is a blessing. I need my strong, handsome and confident Mikey back. What will I do when I'm weak or vulnerable and need to draw strength from you? Not only that, why cheat our children out of the opportunity to watch their father play the game that he still loves, and be proud of you? I can sit here all day and give you reasons why you should get your act together, but you have to want it baby. Success never comes easy. You've spent most of your life working hard to play professional football. Now the only person in your way is you. What is it going to be? Are you a quitter?"

"I need to be alone right now. I'll pick you up at Robin's later."

"We rode in the same car."

"I know. I'll have my trainer drop me off when I'm ready to go."

"Okay baby, I'll see you later. Just know that I love you no matter what you decide to do."

I gave him a kiss, then I left him alone. Instead of me going straight home, I decided to stop by Mike's parents' house to discuss his recent behavior. I guess I was hoping that we could collectively get him out of the funk he was in. His father wasn't home, so I sat down with his mother for nearly an hour. I called and let Robin know where I was, just in case he got there before I did. The last thing I needed was to give him something else to complain about. As we sat down to talk, I couldn't help but to admire how beautiful she was, and the way she carried herself. I could see where Kelly got most of her good qualities from.

"You know Keya, I have noticed a change in Mike. It's been going on for quite a while now. Instead of him dressing nice and staying clean cut, he started letting his facial hairs grow in thick, and he stopped sending his clothes to the cleaners. I asked him a million times what was wrong, but he wouldn't confide in me. i knew that it had something to do with you, because he didn't talk about you all the time like he used to. I figured that y'all broke up or something, and then everything came out. He told me what happened and how it affected him. I could see the pain in his eyes. It killed me that there was nothing I could say or do to help him. I was relieved that he was continuing to open up to me. When he told me that he loved you more than he loved himself, I knew that he was making a bad decision. He was about to marry a woman that he didn't love unconditionally. I think Sheila knew it too, and that's why she called it off. The only one that can help him is you. I will assist you in any way that I can. I love my son to death and there's nothing I won't do to help him. Like I said though, you're the one that can get him right."

"I had a long talk with him not too long ago, and I threatened to walk away if he didn't get his act together. I don't know how much good that did. He told me that he needed to be alone and that he would see me later. I don't know if it's a good sign or not."

"That's a great sign. He used to be the same way when he was younger. Whenever he would be stressed out or something was bothering him, his father would have a long talk with him, then he would drift off by himself and be as good as new in no time. You're his voice of reasoning now and your words are taking affect as we speak. Just give him some time and he'll be as good as new."

"I pray that you're right, because stress is the last thing I need in my life. I'm no good to him or anyone else if I'm stressed out."

"That's one of the reasons he'll snap out of it. That's enough about Mike for now, how are you doing?"

"I'm ten times better, and I'm approving every single day. I enrolled back in school so I could achieve my short term goal of getting my degree."

"That's good Keya, I'm proud of you. Please forgive me for not personally coming to see you. I just felt like you needed to be surrounded by family."

"You are family, regardless if I'm with Mike or not. I got all the messages from Kelly. I truly appreciated all the cards and flowers too."

"I'm glad that you feel that way Keya. I didn't want you to think I was choosing sides between you and Sheila. You've always been my favorite. During Mike's game, it wasn't the appropriate time to talk to you like I wanted to."

"You expressed your concern and that was more than enough for me. We've built a great relationship over the years and I hope I haven't done anything to destroy that."

"Mike told me about him walking in on you and that guy. I told him that time heals all wounds, but I want to share something with you. Mike and Kelly don't know about this, so I'm speaking to you woman to woman."

"Whatever you tell me is between me and you," I assured her.

"Mike's father cheated on me years ago. I came home early from work and found him in our basement making love to another woman. Keya, I went ballistic. I put him out and threw all of his things out as well. When Mike and Kelly asked me where their father was, I lied and told them he was away at work. For three long months, I kept asking myself how he could betray me like that. As I continued to dig for answers it dawned on me that I created the problem. Nights that he wanted to make love I denied him; most of the time I complained about being too tired. I eventually talked to him and we never looked back. My reason for telling you that is because things happen, and we make bad decisions. Sometimes those decisions are forced on us. Don't let your past mistakes stop you from having a great future. If there's anything that I can do for you, please don't hesitate to ask. I mean that from the bottom of my heart."

"Thank you so much. I'm glad we had this opportunity to talk. It felt good getting to spend some time with you. I have to go so I can meet Mike. I promise to keep you up to date on what's going on with him too."

I rushed home hoping that Mike was there so we could go relax and talk further. I was assuming that part of his frustrations was because we weren't having sex, and if that was the case, I was going to explain to him that I needed time. He had to understand and respect that. When I finally made it home, there were no sign of Mike, nor did he call. I paged him a few times, but I got no answer. Two hours had gone by, and still no word from him. Now I was starting to worry. I called his mom and Kelly to let them know that I still haven't heard from him, and they promised to let me know if they did. I fought my sleep as much as I could, until my eyelids got too heavy. I paged him one more time, waited for fifteen minutes, then I got in bed and went to sleep.

I had a terrible dream that Mike tried to kill himself, but before I could see if he went through with it or not, I jumped up out of my sleep. I got up to put on my clothes so I could drive around and search for him. I didn't have a clue where I would look, I just knew that I had to do something. I was in a state of panic trying to put my shoes and jacket on. As I walked back towards my bed to grab the car keys off the nightstand, Mike was laying on the other side of my bed sleeping like a baby. I started to wake him up to ask him where he been, but I let him sleep in peace. I looked at the clock, which read 6:22am. I ditched the idea of calling Kelly and her mom until later. I got back in bed and slept like a baby with my man. When we woke up later that day, I was all over him about his whereabouts, and why he didn't return any of my calls. I didn't mention anything about my dream of him attempting to kill himself.

"Slow down baby. You don't have to be so aggressive. I was at the gym all night with my trainer. I'm way behind schedule with my rehabilitation, so I have to put in the hours to get myself right."

"Wow, this is sudden, but I'm loving it."

"What?"

"This new, energized you. I'm afraid to ask what or who brought this out of you."

"Let's just say that I'm very determined for my children to watch me play."

"Oh, okay."

"I have to go grab me something to eat real quick, then I'm on my way to the gym. If you need me, that's where I'll be."

He gave me a quick kiss and ran out the door. I was so relieved that he was willing to get his life back on track. Instead of calling his mother, I went to tell her the news personally.

"Hey Keya, good afternoon. Did you ever get in touch with Mike?"

"Yes, but let me tell you about my horrible dream. He was at the gym with a gun to his head, contemplating killing himself. I woke up out my sleep before anything could happen. I was prepared to drive around looking for him, but he was in my bed sleeping like a baby. That's not it though. I asked him where he was all night, and he told me that he was at the gym with his trainer. You were right though. I do have the power to get through to him. I swear to you, I haven't seen him this energetic since our high school days. He has that youthful spirit again."

"There was never a doubt in my mind. A mother knows their child, and I know where his heart is, and has always been. When he was engaged to Sheila, I told him to make sure he was certain before he took that step. I didn't want him to risk going through a messy divorce. When he was in the hospital in Cincinnati, he confided in me about still loving you. I know you've been through a lot. Don't put too much pressure on yourself thinking you have to rush into anything to please him. He's not going anywhere. Keep focusing on loving yourself first, and just being there for him mentally and emotionally."

"I truly appreciate you Mrs. Carson, because you have always given me sound advice. When I was in the hospital, a major part of my healing process consisted of me loving myself first, and then learning to cope with people. I can't say that I'm one hundred percent healed, or if I'll ever be for that matter, but I do love myself unconditionally. I feel like I'm strong enough to help Mike through his trials and tribulations. In some ways I feel like I owe it to him to be strong, and help him get through any ordeals. Lord knows, he's been there in my corner for years. I'll take it even further by saying he's been my rock since the first day he approached me in high school. There's nothing that I wouldn't do for him. I never told anyone this, but one of the reasons I tried to kill myself was because I thought I destroyed my relationship with him. I couldn't live with that, especially knowing that I hurt him the way I did. As I began to heal, I realized that there were so many ways to have an impact on people's lives, without needing any real effort. It was important, a must for me to get better, because I had to stand up and be accountable. Now look, just some simple words from the heart has given him motivation."

"You're absolutely right. Now just think about what his life, and all the people that love you lives would be like had you left us tragically. Once you get to a certain point or a certain stage in life, you no longer just live for yourself. It might not always show up on the surface, but there's usually someone out there that looks up to you. Someone who you have a major influence on, and that person can be young or old. You inspire me by your strength and your ability to fight and win the toughest battles. Not everyone can do that Keya. It's important to conduct yourself in a way that you see fit. The smallest things we do, can make a big impact on someone's life. Once again, even though I'm older than you, I learned to be strong in every aspect from watching you overcome your adversities. Everything you have gone through is for a reason Keya. What reason, I can't answer that, but it's true. You just have to trust and believe in God. Now you just have to decide what to do with all the useful information that you have."

I wanted to ask her exactly what she meant by a lot of the things she said, but knowing Mrs. Carson, I knew she would tell me that all the answers were within me. I stopped by the gym to check Mike out, but he was working hard and I didn't want to disturb him. I knew my next mission was a long shot, but I still rode to see if I could somehow get in to see Jessica and the other girls. To my surprise, Dr. Meeks greeted me with a smile.

"What took you so long to come back and see us?" She asked.

"I don't know. I honestly didn't think I would be permitted to come back in."

"Why would you think that? I'm your doctor."

"No, No Dr. Meeks. I know that I'm allowed to see you. I was hoping that I could see Jessica and the others. I made them a promise that I would stay in touch, and I don't ever want them to think I lied to them."

"Well, being that I'm the boss, I can arrange that if I wanted to."

"Will you?"

"Well it all depends."

"Depends on what?"

"On you."

"Whatever I have to do just name it. There's nothing I wouldn't do for them."

"Showing up here is more than enough Keya. They would love to see you. Jessica talks about you all the time. Sometimes she makes me think you're still here."

"Jessica is a sweet girl."

"And she loves and looks up to you Keya. Whatever you do, don't disappoint her."

"I promise you I won't."

"I believe you. Let me go take care of everything so you'll be cleared to come in and visit."

"Thank you so much Dr. Meeks."

I had to sit and wait for an hour because of all the channels she had to go through to get me clearance. As I can recall, when a visitor came, they had to make sure all the patients were accounted for. Jessica was the first one to walk in the visiting room.

At first sight of her, I couldn't hold back my tears. Tears poured from her eyes as well. She looked a whole lot better than the last time I saw her. The stress and the pain wasn't a constant in her face anymore. I gave her a big hug, and we enjoyed our private time before the others came.

"Wow, you look so good Jess," I told her through sobs.

"Thank you. I miss you so much. I just sent you a letter yesterday letting you know that I'm getting out of here in a few weeks. There's one small problem that I have Keya."

"What is it? I'll do whatever I can to help you."

"I have to be honest with you, I'm scared. How was it for you when you got out?"

"I was afraid when I first got out too. I felt real uncomfortable, but as time went by, being surrounded by my friends and family helped."

"My mom is all the family that I really have out there and-."

"That's not true Jess. I'm your family too, and I have a strong support team that will provide you with that same love. It's a Sisterhood that I would love for you to be a part of. So what do you say?"

"I would love that Keya. I look up to you and I want to be around you as much as possible, so I can learn how to be strong like you. You're everything that I want to be."

"I appreciate the kind words, but you're going to be stronger than I am, and live whatever life you choose to live. All it takes is loving and having confidence in yourself, then everything else will fall in place."

The others finally came out and more tears followed. I didn't realize how much I missed everyone, until I was in their presence. It felt like a homecoming for me, because these were the same women that I obtained my strength, courage and motivation to move forward from. I just hoped and prayed that each and every one of them ended up with the same results as I have. I made it my job to remind them that it was a day to day, lifetime battle they were facing. As long as they kept that in mind and approached life on a daily basis, the odds were in their favor, in our favor. The reality of the matter was that some people became products of their environment. I was almost a statistic. I just kept preaching on how it was going to be a work in progress, and that we must submit our will to God and not be afraid to change. Most of them didn't have a place to go or know what they would do once they got released, so I offered to give them money to get a fresh start. I still had about forty thousand dollars left from the money I stole from Slim, and giving it to those in need was a good cause. I stayed until dinner, and then we said our goodbyes. As I was leaving Jessica called out to me.

"Hey Keya!"

"What's up Jess?"

"You mean see you later right?"

"Yeah, I'll see y'all later."

I rode home feeling like the world had just been lifted from my shoulders. It was good seeing the girls and knowing that they were all doing well. They all looked like they were at peace. Jessica telling me that she was coming home was good news too. I couldn't wait to introduce her to everybody. I was certain that they would instantly fall in love with her as I did. The great spirit that she had demanded that. As I pulled up in front of the house, I noticed Mike's car was there. I was hoping everything was okay with him, because I was expecting him to still be at the gym or perhaps with the fellas.

"Where have you been?" He asked, as soon as I walked in the door.

"You were busy when I stopped by the gym, so I went to the hospital I was at to go visit Dr. Meeks, and all the girls I was there with."

"You could've at least called me back when you saw that I paged you."

I grabbed my purse from off the couch to search for my pager. I noticed that I had nine different pages, which five of them came from Mike. The other four were from Robin, Melissa, Kelly and Janet.

"Baby I'm sorry about that. I wasn't allowed to take my purse or any electronic devices inside the building with me, and I didn't hear it when I got in the car because I had it on vibrate."

"I was calling to let you know that we're going out to eat tonight."

"Okay, that's cool with me, but I don't mind cooking if you want."

"Nope, we're eating out tonight. I thought it would be a good idea to get all the family together and have a good time. It's been a long time since we all hung out together."

"Oh okay, so this is going to be a family affair?"

"Sure, why not?"

"I mean, I don't have a problem with it. I just wish I knew in advance so I could've gotten my hair and nails done. It would've been nice to go buy me something to wear too."

"How did I know you would say that? Don't you worry about nothing, leave everything up to me. You have an appointment right now. The rest of your crew is already there. As soon as you're ready I can drop you off. Everything else you'll need is in the bedroom"

"I can't believe you got everything planned out like this. It must really be a big occasion tonight. Did the doctor tell you your knee was healed?"

"No, that's not it. We all just need to relax and have a little fun."

"I agree, it's been a minute since I had some fun. I'm ready to go when you are."

Everybody was already in the chair when I got there, so by the time I was finished getting my manicure and pedicure, it was time for me to get my hair done. I told myself that I needed to have Mike schedule all my appointments from now on. Today was a record time in the hair salon. An hour and a half tops, and I was on my way home to get dressed. I couldn't believe my eyes when I saw the blue Versace dress and shoes on my bed. Something had to be going on, because he went all out. I tried to pry it out of Robin, Kelly, Melissa and Janet, but they were just as clueless as I was. We were all going to know sooner or later, so I took my bath and got dressed. When I walked downstairs and entered the living room, Mike was standing there with his mouth wide open.

"Baby, you look beautiful," he said with a straight face.

"Thank you, I feel beautiful. Where's Robin and Ty at?"

"They left a little early so they could take Monteea to Ty's mom's house. They'll be at the restaurant by the time we get there."

We drove to Mt. Washington and pulled up in front of Monterey Bay, where the valet waited to take our car. Once inside, we were led to a private dining area, where there was music playing and people talking. I had to stop so I could get a clear observation of everything. I noticed that Melissa was there with the rest of the cheerleading squad. Robin, Kelly and Janet were all there with their men. A lot of Mike's friends were in attendance. Even Mike's parents, Momma Sue and Mr. Damon were there. For Momma Sue and Mr. Damon to fly in, something big had to be going down. As I continued to walk around and greet people, and accept all the wonderful comments on how nice I looked, I saw something that totally took me off guard. It was Dr. Meeks, accompanied by Jessica and all the women that I was at the hospital with; my sisters that I went through the struggle with. They were all looking so peaceful and beautiful as ever. I walked over towards them as tears of joy ran down my cheeks. It was a good thing that I didn't wear make-up.

"What are you guys doing here?" I asked, still in disbelief.

"We can leave if you want," Dr. Meeks said with a smile.

"No, I didn't mean it like that. I'm just surprised to see everyone here."

"We're all a part of you," Dr. Meeks responded.

"Yeah, and I told you we would see you later," Jessica said, with an innocent smile on her face.

"Well how did y'all know to specifically come here? Something's going on and y'all know what it is. What's going on?" I continued to dig.

"I invited them," Melissa said, as everyone started to gather around us. "We're all connected from the hip Keya," she continued. "A chain is only strong as its weakest link, and I felt it was a good time to welcome them into our Sisterhood."

"So is that what all this is about?" I asked.

"Maybe, maybe not, but we can use this time to bond and become an unbreakable chain. I know how much these women mean to you, and this is our way of showing you what you mean to us."

"Thank you Melissa. I can't begin to tell you how much this means to me. I love you so much. I love all of y'all," I said in between tears.

They had already met most of the people there, but I took the liberty of re-introducing them, and expressing what they meant to me. Especially Mike, who they felt like they already knew, because of how much I talked about him while I was there with them. We continued to walk around mingling with the rest of my family and friends, until Mike got on the microphone and asked me to join him where he was.

"Some of you already know, but Keya, the reason why we're here tonight is because I have a few things that I want to say to you."

"It took all of this to do that?" I asked.

"Baby please, just relax for a second and hear me out. The first time that I laid eyes on you I knew my life would change, I just didn't know to what degree it would change. I followed my instincts and luckily, by the grace of God, I found my soulmate. Thank you so much for not denying me this opportunity. I also want to say that I love you from the bottom of my heart, and I want to spend my last days within the confines of your love. I got everyone together tonight to express my love in front of our family, friends and loved ones, and to ask you if you'll marry me."

"I don't know what to say Mike. I wasn't prepared for you to ask me to marry you."

"Just say yes, you know you want to," Jessica screamed out through the crowd.

Everyone laughed in harmony, and then got quiet again to hear my response.

"Just express to me how you feel," Mike told me, with a nervous looked on his face.

"Okay, I can do that. I just need everyone to be patient with me and hear me out for a second. This is an emotional time for me, and I need to gather myself. There are times when you can turn a terrible situation into a great one, and that is what has happened since all of you have been acclimated into my life. And you Mike; after all the things that I put you through, that we have gone through, and to still have you here with me, I wouldn't want to share my life with anyone else. Now as far as if I want to marry you. No, because most marriages end in divorce, but I would love to become one with you and be your queen until my time is up here on earth. If we continue to love one another unconditionally like we always have, communicate more and have a mutual understanding, our bond will never be broken. So to clearly answer your question; I'm saying no to marriage, but I would love to walk down the aisle to become one with you."

7He placed the sparkling four carat ring on my finger, kissed me passionately, then pulled me into his arms. Afterwards everyone congratulated us, then we ate and danced the night away. I couldn't have been in a better place. I was surrounded by all the people that I loved and cared for, and who felt the same way about me. Momma Sue grabbed me by the arm while I was dancing in a circle with the girls, and asked me for some alone time. She had a glow in her eyes that let me know she was in a cheerful mood. It had been a long time since I saw that look, and I was happy to be part of the reason it was back.

"Baby I am so happy for you," she told me. "I've been fighting off my tears all evening. I knew he was the perfect man for you the day he brought you home when you were in school fighting."

"I can't believe you still remember that. It was so long ago."

"Hell yeah, that's the only reason why I didn't put that belt to you," she said with a smile. "When you get time, you need to thank him."

We laughed for a little while, and then we grabbed our men and hit the dance floor. As the night began to wind down, Dr. Meeks informed me that it was time for them to leave. I hugged all my sisters, and assured them that I would be coming to see them in a few days.

When it was time to leave Mike was too tipsy to drive, so I took the honors of getting behind the wheel. I didn't drink; I was on a natural high. As I pulled up in the driveway of my new home, I had the task of getting Mike out the car, up the stairs, and tucked in bed. I successfully completed that task, threw on something more comfortable, and then went downstairs to clean up. When I was done, I sat down and reflected on everything that took place at dinner. It was the best and happiest time of my life, a day that I wish I could replay over and over for the rest of my life. As I glanced at the ring on my finger, I couldn't control my emotions and the tears began to pour out. I just kept telling myself that out of all the things that have taken place in my life, the humiliation I put people through, and to still be loved as I am by my family and friends was overwhelming. I couldn't ask for a better life or better individuals to surround myself with. I took a deep breath, soaked everything in one last time, and then I went to bed.

I woke up in the morning to a message from Mike. He informed me that he was at the gym, and that he'd be home around five or six. I didn't have a clue about what I would do until then, so I thought of a few scenarios while I fixed me some breakfast. As I was whipping me up some scrambled cheese eggs and toast, my pager hit the floor from vibrating. I picked it up and took a quick peak at it to see that it was my Uncle Greg paging me 9-1-1. I hurried and put my eggs and toast on a plate, then called him up.

"What's up Unc?" I asked in a worried tone.

"Momma Sue told me about you and Mike, where are you?"

"I'm at Mike's house. I mean, I'm at home eating breakfast."

I gave him the address, then I gobbled down my food while it was still warm. As I prepared to do the dishes, the sparkle from my ring stopped me in my tracks. I still couldn't believe after all that I've been through, that me and Mike was really engaged. I sat back down at the kitchen table and just stared at the ring, while my mind drifted off. My mind took me back to when we first met, our first kiss and how I instantly fell in love with him. Mike was always a true gentleman and he never let his ego get the best of him. That was very rare for a guy of his caliber. The ringing of the doorbell took me out of my daze right when I was thinking about the time we had sex in the rain. It was the first time that I thought about sex since I was raped. I wanted to kill my uncle for interrupting my pleasant thought. Out of spite, I made him wait an extra minute or two.

He gave me a big hug when I opened up the door for him. When he released me from his embrace, I took the opportunity to show off my ring. I was smiling from ear to ear, and so was he, because we both knew that my heart was always with Mike.

"I know he's going to make you happy, he always has. This is a much bigger stage Keya. You're about to share his last name, which means that you can't run to me, Momma Sue or any of your girls when there's a problem or y'all don't agree on things. Communication is the key to a lasting relationship. I know this because I got four different women that I'm involved with, and it requires for me to do a lot of creative management. They all understand that I'm the king, and all servants are to bring me gold or anything of value."

"Listen at you talking all that stuff. You need to stop playing with those women."

"I'm just talking smack. On the serious side, you got to have an understanding with him at all times, and vice versa. There's going to be tough moments, but that's when it's important to reflect on everything y'all been through and build off that. Just focus on trusting your heart and the rest will fall in place."

"I know Uncle Greg; I could've easily done that in the past and lived the perfect life like I believe I'm about to. It wasn't in the cards for me to go that route. It was God's plan for me to go through what I did. Why, I can't explain, but he brought Mike back into my life and I'm mentally, physically and emotionally stronger than I ever been. Of course, it was a rough road for me, but I found a way to survive."

We talked a little longer, and then he took me to get my car. I went to see Monteea and Keesha for a little while then I spent some time with Momma Sue and Mr. Damon, because they were going back home in the morning. We cried our tears of joy, said our I love you's, and then I went home to fix dinner for my man. I had plans of going all out, since this was our first meal together living under the same roof. As I pulled up in the driveway and got out the car, it dawned on me that I didn't have a key to the house. How could I be so stupid not to get the key from Mike? There's no way I could drive to the gym, get the key from Mike, and then drive back home and have dinner ready in time. Frustrated, I jumped back in my car and sat there for a second. I put the key in the ignition and noticed the two gold keys on my ring. I breathed a sigh of relief and smiled, because he always had all the answers. Considering it was him, I was supposed to check my key ring immediately. I got back out my car, used my key because only the door lock was on, and I took me a hot shower before I got his food ready.

I threw on my pajamas that I grabbed from the house, along with all my other stuff that I could fit in my car, and went downstairs to cook. Momma Sue taught me, Robin and Janet how to throw down in the kitchen. The smile on Mike's face when he came home and ate told me that I still had it. He sat with me while I did the dishes, then we went to bed. I played in my hair in the mirror until I got it in a tight ponytail, and I joined him in bed as soon as I was finished. He sat up and looked me in my eyes.

"I'm not going to pressure you or rush you into having sex baby. The most important thing for me is that we're here together."

"I appreciate you being considerate, but I've always felt safe with you. I wouldn't have accepted the ring if I wasn't totally ready to be with you in every aspect."

With that being said, we made slow, passionate love until we fell asleep.

CHAPTER 6

Through hard work and plenty of determination, Mike had successfully completed his rehab and was finally cleared to play football again. That meant that we had to move to St. Louis. Being that Mike got hurt in the pre-season of his rookie year, he never had the opportunity to find a house. We had to stay in a hotel for three weeks, until we found something we liked. It wasn't inconvenient for me, because I was willing to sleep in a cardboard box, as long as Mike was with me. The house that we found was much bigger than the one in Pittsburgh, which we rented out, but there was no place like home. After we got settled in, everything was cool. Mike took me everywhere, introduced me to a lot of people, and treated me like a queen. All of that eventually changed when training camp came around.

He had to stay at the facility with the team during pre-season, so him being the thoughtful person that he is, made arrangements for Melissa and Janet to come stay with me so I wouldn't be lonely. Robin and Kelly even came and stayed for a few days, but they had to get back to their daughters. We had so much fun in those couple days. Like old times, we did each other's hair, did some of our old cheers, and watched some of our favorite movies. We were all older and had our own lives, but I could never outgrow my sisters. When Robin and Kelly had to leave, I sat on my bed that morning like a sad puppy.

"Do y'all really have to leave?" I asked.

"Sis, you know Teea will have a fit if I'm gone too long. It's not the end of the world though, I'll be back again soon."

"Nothing can keep us apart," Kelly added. "Next time I'll bring Keesha with me so I can stay longer."

"Okay, I love y'all," I told them.

It wasn't the same without Robin and Kelly, but the fun most definitely continued. One evening when we were sitting around watching T.V., I felt my stomach bubbling and cramping up. I didn't pay it any attention at first, but it got so bad one time that I had to vomit. I felt funny the entire night, so Melissa and Janet slept in my enormous bed with me to keep a close eye on me. Early the next morning we went to the hospital. After they ran multiple test on me, I was expecting the doctor to tell me that I was diagnosed with food poisoning, or perhaps a stomach virus, but when she broke the news to me that I was ten weeks pregnant, it blew me away. Don't get me wrong, I was happy, ecstatic or let's just say filled with so much joy. Me and Mike had plans on having kids, but for it to come so suddenly kind of took me back. As I continued to sit and digest the news of being pregnant, it solidified that my life was definitely in its transformation stage. What I mean is that, it was out with the old, and in with the new. I told myself that I had closed all the old chapters of my life, but bringing in a child sealed the deal. Raising a child would take some getting used to, but I had all the confidence in the world that Mike and I would do a great job as being parents. With the exception of my mother when the drugs and alcohol took over, we both were raised in good households. I'm just thinking on the fly, and not really knowing what to expect. One thing that I do know is that my child will never endure or experience the pain that I had. All my trials and tribulations would be a sacrifice for my child's joy. Regardless if I was having a boy or girl, it's my job to love, provide for and nurture my child. That's something that I know I'm qualified to do.

On my way back from the hospital, we were so full of excitement. Janet, with her crazy behind, kept rubbing on my stomach making funny noises.

"Girl stop it! You're so crazy, you know that," I told her.

"I know you're not surprised. You know she was always the live wire in the crew," Melissa added.

"Instead of y'all talking about me, Keya you need to be calling your man and letting him know y'all having a baby."

"I'll wait until he comes home."

"What do you mean you'll wait?"

"I just don't want to bother him while he's in training camp. He needs to focus on playing football."

"Keya are you crazy? Letting him know that he's about to be a father, that can't possibly be bothering him," Janet spoke in a serious tone.

"I just want to wait until he comes home so I can tell him face to face."

"That's fine it's a decision that you have to make. Let me ask you something though."

"I'm all ears."

"Your ears are kind of big," Melissa joked.

"Don't go there," I shot back.

"No seriously," Janet interrupted. "What if he finds out from someone else? Do you know how pissed he'll be if that happened?"

"He'll definitely be pissed off at me. I guess that means you and Melissa have to keep y'all mouth shut."

"I swear to secrecy," Melissa told me.

"What if Robin, Kelly or even Momma Sue let it slip out when you tell them?"

"I'm not telling them. Mike will be gone a month at the most. I can wait until then."

"Okay, you're in charge here. The secret is safe with me," Janet told me, finally giving in.

I had to make sure nobody else found out that I was pregnant. The last thing I needed was for Mike to get the news from someone else and we be at each other's throat. I felt that he needed to focus on football right now, and getting through the pre-season without getting hurt. I know from a lot of our conversations, the injury that he suffered the previous year was still in the back of his mind. Getting through the pre-season would boost his confidence. In the meantime, all I needed to do was stay healthy and stress free for the sake of our child, then share the good news with Mike when he came home.

I was almost fourteen weeks pregnant when Mike finally came home. I didn't want to just come out and tell him that I was pregnant, so I left little clues to see if he picked up on it. When my tactic didn't work I immediately began to get frustrated. Mike went to the bedroom and threw the baby bottle and pampers to the side to make room on the bed. I went downstairs to call Janet, who had just left a few days ago with Melissa. I told her about the clues that I left for Mike and his reaction.

"Keya what's wrong with you?"

"Nothing, I thought he would ask me why the stuff was on the bed."

"You need to stop playing games and just tell him girl."

"You're right. I'm about to tell him right now. I'll call you later."

"I got a strong feeling that you'll be calling me right back."

"Shut up, you don't know me," I said, before I started laughing.

"All too well honey," she said, before joining me in laughter.

I hung up the phone with her and went back upstairs to the bedroom where Mike was. He was laying on the bed with his hands behind his head watching t.v.

"Baby, do I stink or something?" He asked me.

"Not that I know of," I answered honestly.

"You wouldn't know if I did or not, because you haven't been around me for five minutes since I got home.

"Aw, do you miss me baby?"

"Of course I do, come here."

"Wait! Before you start being nasty, I really have something that I need to tell you."

At the sound of those words, Mike tensed up and got quiet. He had a seriousness on his face that told me he was a little worried, as he sat up and waited for me to tell him whatever it was I needed to say.

"Baby, I'm trying to think of the best way I can tell you this."

"I have a suggestion. How about just letting the words come out your mouth."

"Thanks smart ass. We're pregnant."

"Stop playing around and just tell me what you need to tell me."

"I'm serious Mike! I'm pregnant!"

"What! Why didn't you just say that baby? I can't believe it! When did you find out? How many months are you?"

"I'm almost fourteen weeks, which is three and a half months. I found out that I was pregnant almost a month ago. I kept feeling sick, and when I went to the hospital they broke the news to me."

"Baby, why didn't you call and let me know when you found out?"

"Because I wanted you to be home next to me when I told you. I wanted it to be special. The only people that know I'm pregnant are Melissa and Janet, now you. I didn't want to risk telling anyone else and you not hearing it from me first."

"I just can't believe we're having a baby!"

He got up off the bed and wrapped me up in his arms. Our mouths connected, and we began to make passionate love. I don't know if it was because of the baby, our body chemistry seemed to be more radiant. Sparks flew all around the room as we explored each other's bodies with great intensity. When our love-making was over, he got up and served me my food in bed, and then we called all our friends and family, giving them the good news. Momma Sue and Jessica was the most excited out of everybody. Momma Sue literally cried when I broke the news to her. It really hit home with Jess about how I truly felt about her when I asked her to be the godmother of my child. Melissa was my original choice, but with Jessica being home now, this would give her a sense of love and responsibility. It wouldn't give her as much time to dwell on the past.

Momma Sue told me that life was finally shaping out to be, how it was always meant to be for me. The rest of the Sisterhood was happy for me and Mike as well. Our phones continued to ring throughout the day with questions about the baby, so it wasn't until late when we finally made it to bed for round two.

As time moved along, things were going smooth for us. My stomach was starting to get bigger and Mike made sure I ate healthy most of the time. I couldn't be denied my ice-cream, peanut butter cookies and my Cool Ranch Doritos. He gave me what we called; my cheat day, to eat those things. The further along I got in my pregnancy, the stronger my bond with Mike became. It was no surprise because he was always there for me since day one, but everything was much more intense now.

Momma Sue always told me, Robin and Janet that where there's joy, comes pain, and I found that out when the happiness I was experiencing was interrupted by a disturbing phone call from her. I was over six months into my pregnancy, but the pain that shot through me made me feel like I was in labor. The call came to me at a quarter to four in the morning. When I heard the seriousness in Momma Sue's voice on the other end, I knew something terrible had happened. Until she actually came out and said what it was, I thought it had something to do with Mr. Damon.

"Keya, I really don't know how to tell you this."

"Momma Sue, what's wrong?"

"Something terrible has happened."

"What is it? Tell me."

The more she continued to procrastinate about telling me what was going on, the more convinced I was that it could possibly be something that happened with one of my sisters.

"It's Eddie and Kenny."

"What have they done now?" I asked, prepared to hear her tell me they were in jail again.

"They were in a car accident."

"A car accident! I don't understand, who was driving?"

"Eddie was driving. They were in a stolen car. Neither one of them made it."

"No! Please tell me I'm dreaming?"

"I wish I could Keya. They crashed into an eighteen wheeler near Greensburg Pike."

"Why! Please God, tell me why!"

"Baby what's wrong?" Mike asked, waking up out of his sleep. "Why Mike! Why?"

He kept asking me what was wrong, but I continued to go crazy, totally ignoring him. When he realized that he wouldn't get an answer from me, he grabbed the phone out my hand.

"Hello!"

"Hi Mike, this is Momma Sue. Eddie and Kenny were in a car accident. Apparently, they had a stolen car and collided head on with an eighteen-wheeler. They were riding on the wrong side of the road ninety-three miles an hour. It was fatal, both of them died instantly."

"Damn y'all! I'll take care of everything here, and we'll be there in a day or so."

"Okay, thanks Mike. Me and Damon are leaving in the morning. If you need me between now and then, call me on my cellphone."

"No problem."

"Tell Keya that I love her and that we'll get through this together."

"I will."

After he got off the phone with Momma Sue, Mike tried his best to calm me down. He told me that I needed to get some rest, but I couldn't sleep. I didn't get any sleep until we got on the plane to go to Pittsburgh. A part of me still didn't believe that my brothers were gone, that was until I talked to my Uncle Greg. I could hear the pain in his voice. He kept the conversation short, I guess to keep me from hearing the weakness in his tone, and risk having me break down. I wasn't the same Keya though. I cried initially, but instead of me constantly crying and feeling sorrow for myself and them, I said my goodbyes through prayer, and I thanked God for opening his arms and welcoming them. After the funeral services, everybody went to my Uncle Greg's house to eat and spend a little time together.

"They were some sweet boys," an elderly lady from next door spoke. "They always came by to empty my garbage, and cut the grass on the weekends. I miss them babies so much."

"I loved them too, and it was an unfortunate situation," another neighbor expressed. "Let's just be thankful that they're in God's hands now," she continued.

"Maybe this was God's plan to prevent them from going through more pain," I found myself saying. "The truck driver had minor injuries, so it's a blessing that more lives weren't lost in the process. We all love and miss them, but we can't ignore the fact that they were headed down the wrong path. God felt that it was time to intervene, and now they're at peace. I also want to say that it feels good to be amongst family and friends. The only problem that I have with all of this is that we shouldn't wait until a tragedy occurs for us to come together like this. If all the love I feel in the air is real, let's be in the company of each other more, because it's in our hearts. I can't speak for everyone else, but I personally want to be showered with love from my friends and family."

"God bless you child," the elderly woman said, as she got up to hug me. "I understand where you're coming from, because we use to have family reunions every year. Close friends would also come. It's not like that anymore. I don't know what happened to the generations."

"The streets swallowed them whole," another friend of the family jumped in.

"Together, we can bring back those good old days," I shared.

As the day began to dwindle away, the rest of the evening went well. Me and Mike went home a few days later, and I felt at peace saying goodbye to my brothers, because I knew they were at peace. I assured Mike that me and the baby were okay, and that helped calm his nerves.

"You're missing your true calling," Mike told me.

"What's that supposed to mean?" I asked him.

"You're an excellent speaker, with a whole lot to say."

"I just speak from the heart baby."

"That's what makes it even better. You have a great story."

"What do you mean? A great story in regards to my life?"

"That's exactly what I'm talking about."

"I feel too ashamed to talk about my past to people."

"Why? It's an amazing story how you overcame all that you have."

"Right now, you and our child are all that I'm focusing on."

"I'll let it go for now, but we'll be re-visiting this conversation in the near future."

Mike would occasionally bring that topic up, but it wouldn't last long, because I refused to respond. His team wasn't doing so well, and their chances of making the playoffs ended week eleven into the season. I felt sorry for him because they had big expectations, but as he sat home and watched the playoffs, he finally had something to feel good about. On January 26th, at 10:47p.m, our beautiful daughter came into this world weighing seven pounds and six ounces. Mike was so attached to her that I felt jealous. I guess I felt the way I did because my father never gave me that love and affection.

Everybody was there to support and congratulate us. Being that we agreed months ago that Mike would name our daughter, I was a little nervous not having a clue what name he would choose. When he chose the name Karen, it totally blew me away. Before I could ask, he was giving me his explanation.

"During our intimate talks, I could tell that your mom was a good person before the drugs and alcohol. I never had a chance to meet her, but I saw it in your eyes there was once love there, and that you missed those loving moments. With that being said, our daughter will represent the goodness in your mother. I hope that's not a problem."

"Absolutely not. You always go to the extreme to show me how much you love me, and I am so fortunate to have you. Baby I wouldn't trade you or this moment for nothing in the world."

So it was official. We named our daughter Karen Monique Carson. Every single time I looked at my beautiful princess, only the good memories of my mother surfaced. I didn't have to worry about my poor excuse of a father coming around wanting to be a part of her life, because he was a full time dope fiend, going back and forth to jail. Mr. Damon was the only grandfather she needed to know on my side of the family, and Mike's parents were the best as well. They never told us why, but giving birth to Karen in Pittsburgh meant a lot to them.

Since the football season was over, we decided to stay in Pittsburgh for a while. It was important to both of us to spend as much time as we possibly could with our friends and family. They were intricate parts of our lives. Plus I didn't want to be a hypocrite after the speech I gave the day of my brother's funeral, about not using tragedies as an excuse or the only reason everyone came together. We ended up staying in Pittsburgh over four months, then we headed back home to St. Louis. When Mike was scheduled to start training camp, he told me that I could go visit Momma Sue until pre-season was over.

"Me and Karen will just stay home so we can be close to you."

"The only communication that we'll have is phone calls, and you can still receive the same phone calls wherever you are."

"Is there something else I need to know? Are you trying to get rid of me?"

"Stop playing. You can stay home if you want, it's your choice. I just didn't want you to be in the house lonely."

"What difference does it make? You're gone during the season too."

"It's only for a few days, but during pre-season I'm gone over a month."

"You're right."

He made a valid point, so I made plans to go visit Momma Sue and Mr. Damon for a few weeks. Even as I was boarding the plane, I was questioning my decision. I dreaded it a little because Momma Sue was quick to give her input on everything, and she didn't sugarcoat nothing. I was sure she'd find something to constructively criticize me about, and I really wasn't in the mood for her digging into me, but I went anyway.

The moment we stepped inside the house, Momma Sue immediately went into mother mode. She took Karen off my hands, and provided her with the love and nurturing that she was missing. It didn't have anything to do with how good or bad I was as a parent; Momma Sue was just more experienced than I was. Karen was my top priority even over myself, she was happy and very healthy. I know I was doing an excellent job.

"How's grandma's lil' beautiful baby? I said how's grandma's beautiful baby girl? Me love you so much!"

"Momma Sue, there was a time when I thought you was great with children, because of the way you were with me, Robin, Janet and the rest of the kids in the neighborhood. But as I've gotten older and able to understand things, I see that you're just great with people."

"That's kind of funny, because Robin said the same thing to me when she had her daughter. Being good with people, as you say, is not something that I practice at. Well it is practice in a way, because I constantly try to do things that's right, from the heart, and give the respect to people that I want for myself and my family. Keya, when we learn how to be who we are, and stay true to who you are, life becomes easy because we don't have to do things out of the ordinary. Now since we're sitting here having a heart to heart, what are your plans.?"

"My plans on what?"

"Your plans on life. Do you plan on sitting around and making babies, or do you have goals that you hope to achieve?"

"I never thought about living a particular life. I guess I just always wished to live comfortably, and I'm doing that. Me and Mike own nine houses, eight of them we rent out, plus the money he makes playing football."

"Okay, money's not a problem. What about your personal goals? Do you have any?"

"My personal goals now are being able to focus on being as supportive as I can to Mike and Karen."

"So you mean to tell me that all you care to do is be supportive to Mike and your daughter? Don't get it confused, there's absolutely nothing wrong with that, but there's still room for you to do something for yourself. Keya, you have a college degree. Why let it go to waste?"

"Do you want the truth?"

"Always."

"I'm afraid to come out of my comfort zone. I know that life can always be better than it is, but I'm content, I'm in my comfort zone. I went through so much to get where I am now, and I don't want nothing to get in the way of that. I'm afraid to step out and possibly failing. I don't ever want that feeling of rejection or defeat again."

"I know exactly what you're going through. I was there once upon a time, and like you, I was afraid to fail. I had a chance to pursue a modeling career. It was a long shot, because I was always thick and the traditional model was slim and tall. I didn't want to go up against the odds, so I used the excuse of having to take care of you and Robin. I regret that decision now, because I always ask myself what if. I'm pleased with the life I have, but how can we succeed if we don't even try?"

"You're right, but I'm afraid to go back down that road of misery."

"I think you're being a little over dramatic."

"I wouldn't say that I'm being over dramatic. Maybe cautious would be the best word to use."

"I can go back and forth with you about which words are appropriate or not. The bottom line is that you can't live your life for someone else. Don't look back on life one day, and regret that you didn't pursue your goals and dreams."

"I understand everything that you're saying. At this present time, life is complete for me. You have people out there that have successful careers, but some of them can't handle the pressures that come with the territory. Some people turn to drugs and alcohol, they commit suicide, you name it, and the list goes on. I can honestly tell you that I'm happy Momma Sue. I have the man of my dreams, a beautiful daughter, family and friends that love me like I love them, and I'm financially stable. At the end of the day, ain't that what it's all about?"

"I guess. If that's what you really want, and you can live with it, I'm happy for you. It's just my job to bring out the best in you and Robin. I love y'all with all my heart, and I just want my babies to be okay."

"I love you too Momma Sue, and we will be okay, because if nothing else, we have each other. I'm at peace with myself now, and I don't want to jeopardize that with what ifs."

"I understand honey."

I ended up staying with Momma Sue and Mr. Damon for almost two months. Mike called me every single day, but it still didn't fill the void of not having him at home with us. I missed my baby so much. I needed to smell, touch and taste him badly. Momma Sue must've sensed that I was missing Mike. She took me and Karen out daily, showing me around or shopping to help me take my mind off him. Her plan worked and my days began to fly by.

A few weeks into my visit with Momma Sue, we got a surprise visit from Robin, Monteea, Kelly, Keesha, Janet, Melissa, Jessica and the rest of my Sisterhood. It felt good seeing all of them.

"Wow, what made all of y'all come here? The last time we all got together like this, Mike asked me to marry him. Is there another special occasion that I don't know about?"

"We all needed a vacation for a few days, and we have a wedding to plan," Robin told me.

"Oh yeah, and who's idea was it to come help me plan my wedding? I think it's more to it than you're telling me."

"Stop being so suspicious all the time. It was all of our idea," Robin carried on.

"We don't see the reason why you keep prolonging it. Let's start planning and make this thing happen Sis."

"Since y'all came all this way, let's get it done."

Momma Sue's house wasn't big enough for all of us, so we pitched in for two Presidential suite's that had connecting doors, while Momma Sue agreed to keep the kids. It was the first week of August and everyone thought I should have the wedding in March or April. I chose May, but instead of having it at Mike's family church in Pittsburgh, I wanted my special day to be in Florida or California. After all the votes were in, we chose South Beach. They pretty much had everything else figured out. Melissa already had the wedding planner lined up. She called and gave Torina the general ideas that we had.

"Hey Melissa! I wasn't expecting to hear from you this soon. I think I can come up with something spectacular at a reasonable price. Of course, I would have to fly to South Beach to find a good wedding site, and to reserve it."

"Will that be a problem? Melissa asked.

"I don't see it being a problem."

"Okay thanks. I assured my sister that you were the best money could buy. I have all the confidence in the world that you'll do a great job."

"Thanks Melissa, I really appreciate your confidence in me. Your sister's name is Keya right?"

"Yes."

"Tell Keya that this will be the most beautiful, and memorable day of her life."

"I will, talk to you soon."

Janet and Kelly were in charge of the caterer's, and Robin wanted to design the cake. The only thing left were our dresses. We had plenty of time to take care of that, so we spent the next couple days hanging out and enjoying each other's company. After a week of fun, my company had to leave. It was cool, because me, Momma Sue, Karen and Mr. Damon kicked it. I had so much fun with them, that I seriously thought about getting a house in Charlotte.

Pre-season was finally over. Mike surprised us and came to stay a few days in Charlotte before he took us home. When he came in my room early in the morning, I jumped out the bed and ran to him like I use to run to my father when I was younger. The only difference is that Mike held me tightly in his arms, and I know he'd always be there for me. I can't begin to explain how happy I was to see him. Even though

Karen was only eight months old, you could tell by her constant smile that she missed him too.

"Baby, I missed you so much," I told him, in between pecks on his lips and cheek.

"I missed you too. Just talking to y'all every single day and constantly looking at y'all pictures wasn't enough for me. I needed to hold y'all in my arms."

We both wanted to make love bad, but Mike had too much respect for Momma Sue. I begged him several times in a low whisper, but he still wouldn't give in. We just cuddled for the two days we stayed there. When we got home it was fair game. Unless it was to tend to Karen, use the bathroom or to eat, we didn't get out the bed.

"I don't need you to be gone that long again. We need you home with us."

"You know I can't do nothing about training camp or our away games."

I could deal with the games during the regular season. I already had that calculated to the second. Eight weeks out of the sixteen weeks he would be on the road. It would only be for two days max, unless the weather was bad. So altogether, he would be away sixteen total days for road games. I had it all locked in my mind. As I was doing the math about how long he would be gone, the conversation I had with Momma Sue popped up in my head. Is this the life I really wanted to live? Did I want to be the type of woman that sat around and waited for my man with nothing to do, or did I want to be an independent, confident woman that family and friends could rely on? As I weighed my options in my head, as much as I loved Mike, staying at home barefoot and pregnant just didn't sound like the idea thing to do. One of my mother's downfalls was that she allowed my father and all the other men in her life to control her physically, mentally and emotionally. Had she been head strong and independent, the drugs and alcohol would've never come into the picture. I went through that with Slim, but I couldn't keep sitting around allowing him to beat me whenever he felt the need to put me in line. That's why I took action the way I did. Although Mike is the total opposite from Slim, me not being in control of my daily functions was just as risky as me pursuing my goals and dreams and failing. Maybe Momma Sue was right about me doing something with myself, but after achieving my short term goals, I didn't have any realistic goals and dreams. Maybe I could do some volunteer work for Dr. Meeks when Mike was in training camp, and parts of the season. That was basically all that I could think of, especially since I had trust issues with everyone that wasn't a friend or family. I'm stubborn and being apart from my king and princess right now just ain't in the cards. Until something specific came to mind, I was content with my life the way it was.

Mike had a week off before the season started, so we used that time to mingle with his teammates and their wives or lady friends. As he displayed his charming smile while he proudly showed me and Karen off, I was careful not to wear my feelings on my sleeves. I was lucky I didn't prejudge because I had the wrong impression about those women. I thought all sports athletes' wives were arrogant and stuck on themselves, because they were covered with all the latest fashions and drove foreign cars, but these women were down to earth, and fun to be with. When the season started we took turns watching the games over each other's houses. We kept each other so busy that we hardly missed our men when they were on the road.

Being that Mike was the backup quarterback, he barely played. That didn't stop him from taking his job seriously. He worked hard every week as if he was the starter. The coaching staff recognized his hard work and commitment to the team, and he was rewarded with a four year contract extension that paid him close to nine million dollars. I was happy for him because with the extension, he told me that he finally felt like he made it to the NFL. I didn't and would never tell him that I wanted him to stay a backup, to avoid him from getting hurt. Had I made a comment like that to him, he would've felt betrayed, like I didn't have confidence in him, and I didn't want to travel down that road, so I kept my mouth shut. From spending time with the other players significant others, they all basically felt the same way I did. All any of us could do was silently pray that our men made it home safe every weekend. I knew Mike wanted to be on the field, because football was his life, and he wanted to show us he could play with the best. Unlike the previous year, his team made the playoffs, but they lost in the first round to the New York Giants. With the exception of the quarterback, the St. Louis Rams were a young team on the rise. Mike couldn't stop talking about it.

"I'm proud of my team and how hard we played this year. I hope it carries over into next season, and we make a deeper run in the playoffs. I might get to start next season too, because the team doesn't want to invest a lot of money into an older quarterback. He might get a one or two year deal.

"Whatever happens, just continue to work hard and be ready when your number is called."

"You sound like coach Nox," Mike chuckled.

"I know a little somethin', somethin'," I joked.

"Well that's enough football talk. Are you ready to become Mrs. Carson?"

"I've been ready since the first day we met."

The moment had finally come for me to become Mrs. Carson. South Beach was beautiful, especially for a wedding. I was a nervous wreck. If all my sisters and my mother hadn't been there, I don't know what I would've done with myself. Me and all the bridesmaids wore white, while Mike and the fellas wore white with burgundy trimming. Everything was absolutely perfect. The hardest thing for me was when we said our vows to each other. I prayed that I got through it before I broke down. Lucky for me, Mike went first.

"Keya, you're most definitely the apple of my eye, and the love of my life. I grew up going to church every Sunday and praising God, but as I got older, I had my doubts in his abilities. I constantly prayed to him for things and never received any of them. Finally, I began to see his work during my junior year in high school. That's when I met you. Baby you were a sight for sore eyes. You were confident, and you were also a fashion icon," he said with a smile. "It didn't take long for you to be a part of my soul either. One day I woke up in the middle of the night because my mouth was throbbing, but the pain instantly went away. The next day you missed school because you had a tooth ache. I don't know, maybe we were just extra sweet on each other," he said, cracking another smile. "Baby we are mentally, emotionally, physically and spiritually connected and you taught me to never doubt God again, because there are times that he has better things planned for us, than what we prayed for. I can honestly say that, because I thank him every night for the strong, loving, remarkable woman that I have in you. If I could change one thing in my life, I would go back and make you my wife a long time ago. Baby I never, ever, want to be apart from you. My heart bleeds for you."

"Wow, I never thought I'd see this day. Mike, I went through so much as a child, and it made me cold-hearted and numb. That was until you came along. Honestly, I thought you were a prophet or something. You were the only one who could knock down the wall I had built up, and I was constantly filled with excitement whenever you came around. You were patient with me and now I know that God is a loving and forgiving God, because we fought through thunderstorms, tornadoes, hurricanes, and any other obstacles. Now here we are with a bond that's unbreakable, and a love stronger than ever. Mike, I pledge my life to you; to be your friend, your confidant, your voice of reasoning, understanding, and part of your solid foundation. Until the day I max my time out on this earth, I fully commit to becoming one with you. Without you my soul no longer exists."

At that moment, I became Mrs. Keya Carson. It was one of the happiest moments of my life. I knew me getting married meant a lot to my Uncle Greg, because it was the first time I had ever witnessed him shed a tear. I loved my uncle to death, and together we looked up at the sky and waved, because we knew my mom and brothers were looking down on us with smiles on their faces. The reception was a blast. We had more food than we could possibly eat, great music, and plenty of surprises. Tony Terry came out and sang two songs for us. Me and Mike started things off with the first dance. When Tony Terry chirped "With You," I almost melted in Mike's arms. It was the perfect song, and I felt the power in his words.

"It's-for-real. What-I-feel. When-I'm-with-you."

He finished up with his song Everlasting Love, which was perfect as well, because me and Mike had the kind of love that would last forever. It was a day to remember, and one that I would always treasure.

CHAPTER 7

(5 YEARS LATER)

After performing at a high level the last year of his contract with the St. Louis Rams, Mike earned a starting job with the Cleveland Browns. The paycheck was large, but he had a career ending leg injury his second season with the Browns. During his brief stint with them, the only good thing about our experience in Ohio was the big bucks we got and that it was close to home. The injury that he suffered didn't prevent him from walking or doing normal things, but from a football standpoint it limited his abilities. After seven years in the league he had to hang up his cleats. There was a bright side to it though. Our beautiful daughter Karen was now six years old and grown as ever. Her sister Bria, my other daughter, was four years old. Together they did a great job of keeping him busy; us busy, and we were a complete and happy family.

We eventually moved back home to Pittsburgh and officially began our new life without football. For me it was perfect having Mike home with us every single day and not have to worry about him getting hurt anymore. I never told him about the guilt I felt when he did get hurt, because I always put it in the universe that he would get hurt if he played regularly. It's just something that I had to deal with internally.

In the beginning, not being able to play football was eating him alive. As time went on he eventually began to settle into his new role. He shifted that love and passion he had for playing football over to being active full time in our lives. Mike started loving the idea of being able to take his daughters to school every morning. He left it up to me to get them dressed and fed, then he stepped in. Being that all the staff knew he was a celebrity, they would ask him to hang around sometimes to read books to the kids. He signed his share of autographs as well. That gave me a few hours of free time during the week which I really didn't need because I loved the three of them unconditionally and I never wanted to be apart from them. While Mike was off doing his thing with the girls, I was at home cleaning up the house and listening to my music. I had Whitney Houston's "You Give Good Love," blasting so loud that I barely heard the phone ringing. As I ran across the room to answer it, I didn't like the sound of Jessica's voice.

"Jess what's wrong? I don't like how you sound."

"I have a problem that I need you to help me with!"

"Talk to me. You know there's nothing that I won't do for you."

"I know, I know! It's my cousin Melanie!"

"Okay, that's the one you told me you love like a little sister."

"Right! She had an altercation with some boys at her school! They surrounded her, threw her to the ground, then snatched her underwear off her! They were about to rape her, but luckily someone seen what was going on and went to get a teacher before anything could happen!"

"Oh my God! I'm so sorry to hear that Jess!"

"What pisses me off Key, is that the boys responsible only got suspended for three days! And can you believe that the school never contacted the police?"

"I hope y'all was smart enough to contact them."

"Of course! We got all their names and contacted the police immediately! My cousin is filing a lawsuit against the school too!"

"Okay, that was smart. Can you please calm down now?"

"Okay, I'm taking a deep breath now. I'm good."

"How is Melanie doing now?"

"Keya she's scared to death, and I really don't know what to say to her. I mean I tried, but she really won't say much to me or her mother."

"Did you try to call Dr. Meeks?"

"Calling her never even crossed my mind."

"Why not?"

"Because this is a situation that you can handle. If it wasn't for you and the other girls, I don't know what I would've done or how I would've gotten through my situation."

"Jess that's a totally different situation. We were all vulnerable women who desperately needed each other to get through the adversity we endured. Dr. Meeks is a paid professional that deals with those types of situations for a living."

"The only difference between you and Dr. Meeks is that she gets paid to counsel people and you don't. I don't mean to put you under the gun or bring back painful memories, but you have a way with how you communicate with people. Maybe it was a mistake on my behalf for even calling you with this."

"Wait a minute Jess, it's not like that! I was just making a suggestion to you because Dr. Meeks is qualified."

"I'm desperate right now Key, I need you."

"And you know you can always pick up the phone and call me. That's not a problem."

"Well help us then?"

"I don't mind helping out if I can."

"Thank you so much Key."

"For starters, look into enrolling Melanie into an all-girls school. She's going to feel uncomfortable around boys. Besides that, even though she's not responsive as she should be, y'all have to be there for her because she needs all the love and support she can get right now. Is her father in her life?"

"What! That low life son of a bitch! He takes pride in making babies all across town and not taking care of them!"

"Wow, I'm sorry to hear that. I know the feeling because my biological father neglected me. But back to Melanie; everyone reacts to things differently, so it might take a long time or she might get through it quickly."

"It looks like it might take longer. She won't talk to us at all."

"I'll try to see if I can help, but I don't see her responding to me if she won't communicate with her own family."

"Thanks again Key."

"Do you want to bring her to me or I can come to you."

"It might be better if you came to us. She's spooked out of her mind."

"Okay, give me the address. I have a few things to take care of, then I'll be on my way."

I finished cleaning up the house without the music on, because my thoughts were pre-occupied with what I was going to say to Melanie. I should've convinced Jessica to call Dr. Meeks and left it at that. I always managed to put myself in difficult situations for people I cared about. When I finished cleaning, I got myself together and left Mike a note letting him know where I went.

It took me a little over forty minutes to get there from my house, but I was hesitant on calling Jess and letting her know that I was outside. I wanted to call Dr. Meeks or Melissa to join me. After mentally going back and forth with myself, I made the call to Jess. When I entered the house Jess took me straight to Melanie's room without even introducing me to the mother. I found that odd, but I went along with it and didn't question her about it. Upon entering Melanie's room, we found her sitting in the dark squeezing her pillow tight. The first thing I did when we clicked on the lights was walk over to her and gave her a hug before I said a word. She was well proportioned to be her age and I could see why those horny eighth graders tried to take advantage of her. I wanted to make her feel as comfortable as possible around me, so I had messed my hair up before entering her room and kept a sad expression on my face. After hugging her, she just looked up at me.

"Hi Melanie. My name is Keya. I'm a friend of Jessica's. I came to talk to you, but you don't have to talk if you don't want," I told her.

She just continued to stare at me without saying a word. I started to hug her again because she looked like she could use another one.

"If you ever need someone to talk to, Jessica knows how to get in touch with me," I told her as I got up to walk away.

"They threw me to the ground real hard and-."

"I know, come here. I promise it'll be okay. I won't let nobody hurt you," I said, as I gave her another hug.

"Please don't let them hurt me!" she began to cry.

"I won't Melanie," I whispered. "Do you want to go to a different school?"

"Yes, I don't want to go back there! I'm scared!"

"You don't have to go back there and you don't have to be scared anymore. Can I tell you a story?"

"Yes."

"When I was thirteen years old this man snatched all my clothes off and did bad things to me. I was scared just like you are, but my mom was there and she didn't let nobody bother me no more. You're safe now Melanie. Me, your mom and Jessica will always be here to make sure nobody else bothers you."

"Okay," she said, finally letting go of her pillow and loosening up a little.

I gave her another hug and to my surprise she hugged me back. As I was about to get up to leave the room to talk with Jess and Melanie's mother, she grabbed my hand and held it tightly. I looked at her and noticed tears rolling down her cheeks, so I sat back down on the bed.

"Can you please stay with me?" she asked.

"Sure," I told her.

There was a sigh of relief on her face as she laid her head gently on my lap. I rubbed her back for a second to make her feel comfortable, and then I ran my fingers through her soft black hair as the room remained silent. Jess and Melanie's mom were still in the room with us, but they kept quiet. We all seemed to relax until my cell phone started vibrating and startled Melanie.

"It's okay baby. That's just my phone ringing. You can lay your head back down."

Sitting there comforting her made me think about the days when Momma Sue gave me, Robin and Janet all the love and care we needed. Just on the strength of knowing her situation, I was in it for the long haul with making sure Melanie was okay.

When I answered my phone it was Mike calling to let me know they were home and that he fed the girls already.

"Okay honey, I'm going to be here a little longer than expected. You can bring them to me if you want to."

"Is everything okay?" He asked.

"Yeah, I'll explain everything to you later."

"I can keep Karen with me. She's in her own little world playing in her room. Bria's a different story though. She constantly keeps crying for you, so I'll just bring her to you and keep Karen with me."

"Just bring them both to me. You know Karen will eventually be wanting to come with us."

"I guess you got a point. What's the address?"

"I wrote it down on the note I left for you."

"I never saw a note. Where did you put it?"

"How about looking on the refrigerator where we always leave messages at."

"Hold on smart ass, let me check. Okay I got it. I'm on my way."

When I hung up the phone, I directed all my attention back to Melanie. She was still lying on my lap, but now looking directly up at me.

"What's wrong?" I asked her.

"Nothing," she answered in the cutest child voice.

"Would you like to meet my two daughters'?" I asked.

"Yeah, can I please?"

"Okay, they're on their way. Can I do your hair?"

"Do you know how to braid?"

"Of course I do. I'm a girl and I have two girls."

"I want some braids."

While I was braiding her hair we began to talk about cheerleading and her favorite hobbies. I was surprised when she told me that she loved to play basketball. I just couldn't picture it. She had the perfect body for cheerleading and gymnastics. I told her about my days as a cheerleader and I even showed her a few moves that I could still put down swell. We were having a good ole time, until Jess interrupted us to let me know Mike was outside. When I got downstairs to the door I stopped Mike from coming in. I stepped outside instead.

"Melanie, I'll be right back okay."

"Okay."

"Mommy!" Bria hollered out as I walked to the car.

"What's going on?" Mike asked.

"Some boys tried to rape Jessica's lil' cousin at school."

"Damn."

"She wouldn't talk to nobody at first, but I managed to get her to loosen up. She'll be okay. I'll be home soon."

"Take your time. Me and Ty are headed over to Mont's and Robin's house to go workout a little bit."

"Okay, I love you honey."

Karen ran up and gave Jess a big hug when we entered the house, and then she ran over to speak to Melanie and her mother. Bria wasn't as friendly though. She grabbed onto my leg and wouldn't let go.

Melanie started to loosen up a little more when she started playing with Karen and Bria. It made me feel good to see the relief on Jessica and Melanie's mom's face as they watched her laugh and play with my daughter's. I displayed a bright smile of my own and winked at Jessica.

"You're a miracle worker," Jessica whispered to me.

"No God is a miracle worker," I told her. "He's just working through me."

"I have to believe that he works through people, and I want to have that deep spiritual connection and avoid the past life experiences that I had. And who knows, maybe he'll work through me soon."

"Jess, don't worry about being too deep or not deep enough in your spirituality, because a pure heart doesn't lie. He never puts us in situations that we can't handle. We are living testaments of the miracles he performs. As long as you stay positive and live your life righteously, you'll get your opportunity to work for the almighty. You just have to be ready when your turn comes."

"I'll keep that in mind."

"Excuse me, I don't mean to interrupt, but we've all been so overwhelmed with Melanie that Jessica never introduced us."

"You're not interrupting. As you already know, my name is Keya."

"My name is Jasmine, and it's truly a pleasure meeting you. I am forever grateful to you for helping us."

"There's nothing I wouldn't do for Jess."

"I understand. She told me all about how y'all met, and the impact y'all have on each other's lives. You've been through a lot."

"Yes I have."

"Why not share your testimony with the world and reach out to the women who went through what you did, but don't necessarily have the strength to overcome those hurdles," Jasmine continued. "As a woman of God, I too agree that God performs his works through us, and your work is not done Keya. There are thousands or maybe even millions of women and even little girls out there that need you."

"I never looked at things like that. My main focus has been on my family and keeping our foundation strong. This is just a situation where Jessica called and I came running."

"Again, I am very grateful that you came running, but it's a shame because you have a whole lot to offer. No disrespect intended Keya, but I feel like you're being selfish by only focusing on you and your family. There are so many people that you can be helping. Melanie is a prime example. You spent a few hours with my daughter who wouldn't open up to her own mother, and now she's crazy about you. How often does that type of thing happen?"

"She's right Key, you had the same effect on me. When you got released from the hospital it killed

LOVE'S NOT SUPPOSED TO HURT

all of us, but you left your strength and will behind. It was like a part of us died though."

"I don't know what to say. I really don't."

"That's the thing Keya. You have to be willing to do, in order for you to say," Jasmine continued to push.

"If certain things are meant to be it'll happen. God has a purpose for me; I'm just waiting for his message."

"Listen carefully, because he's trying to communicate with you now," Jasmine told me.

"I will."

Melanie and my daughters began to wear each other down, so I talked to her a little bit before we left and promised to come visit her tomorrow. She nodded her head and crashed out on the couch before I even made it to the door.

"I really, really appreciate you stopping by and taking time out your day to be here for my daughter. I have never seen her gravitate to someone like she has to you. I really think you should give what I was saying some thought."

"I promise I will."

"Trust me Keya. People will respond to you in a positive way, because you're loving, caring and very understanding. We were fortunate to have you, and so were the ladies at the hospital. The sisterhood is so thankful to have you Key. Imagine how the rest of the world will feel," Jessica added. "I honestly thought that I would be scarred for life, but you showed me that life with true love really does exist. I am able to love, trust and be with a man in every way. You used to always preach to us that love's not supposed to hurt, and now I'm experiencing that firsthand with Craig."

"I need to get out of here before I break down and start crying. Since you're twisting my arm Ms. Lady; if I decide to go around speaking you're in it with me."

"I'll be with you every step of the way. As a matter-of-fact, it can be something that the Sisterhood can do together."

"Wow, you might be on something. This type of thing is right up Melissa's alley. We'll see what happens."

"Have a good night Keya," Jasmine said before walking off.

"You have a good night too and I'll see y'all tomorrow. Jess I'll call you as soon as I get home and get the girls settled in."

All the playing Karen and Bria did made them hungry, so we stopped by Wendy's on the way home, because there was no way I was going home to stand in front of the stove. I was too tired to do anything. I got the girls what they wanted and ordered myself a chicken sandwich, small fries and a small drink. We decided to wait until we got home to eat our food. My truck was a total mess. I made a mental note to get it cleaned immediately though. A Range Rover wasn't supposed to look how mines did inside.

When we reached our destination Mike wasn't home yet, so I called to let him know we finally made it home, then I called Jess. I talked to her for a minute and was assured that Melanie was okay, and then I called the rest of my girls and told them about the day I had. Most of them just listened to me talk, but I knew Melissa was going to add her two cents.

"Well, well, well. Didn't we have a talk along those lines years ago? I agree with Jasmine. I believe that God is speaking through other people around you, and he needs you to do more of his work. Honestly, you know what's right and what you have to do. Not just for others, but to continue to make yourself whole. Whenever we hear terrible stories on the radio or see it on television it has an effect on us. I believe we can be a part of the solution. If you need me, you know I'm always here. You know what you have to do."

"I know what's on my heart and yes certain things do affect me even if it doesn't directly affect those I surround myself with. The problem is, I have worked so hard to get where I am in life and I don't want to do anything to compromise myself, my friends or family."

"This is me you're talking to Key. We both know that everything's intact with your friends and family. I think you're just afraid of trying or doing something different. Look at it from a realistic point of view. The worst case scenario is that you can go back to the life you're living now if all fails. What good is love, knowledge, wisdom or anything else if you keep it to yourself?"

"I'm not keeping anything to myself."

"Maybe not, but you're not being helpful to the people that really need you."

"I have to sit down and talk with Mike, then we'll all sit down and talk more."

"Okay, call me."

"I will. Love you Sis."

I didn't get to discuss anything with Mike that night because I was beat from the long day I had, and I crashed before he came home. I was so tired that I slept through the morning. We didn't get a chance to converse until the following afternoon. He got the girls together and took them to school, then went to work out, which gave me the opportunity to sleep peacefully. Even though his football career was officially over he still worked out twice a day, Monday through Friday. We stayed on each other's back about staying in shape. I constantly told him that I needed strong arms to hold me and a pumped chest to lay on. He always laughed, but he knew that I love those two things about him. I placed his lunch in front of him, then sat beside him.

"So what was the outcome from yesterday? Did you get anything accomplished?"

"Surprisingly yes. The young girl's name is Melanie. Some boys tried to rape the poor girl at school. Luckily somebody went and got a teacher before anything happened."

"That's crazy. That comes from people running around making kids and not properly raising them. There are so many young men out there growing up without fathers and they're taking their anger out on any and everyone, particularly girls or women. I can't personally speak about it, but I've seen it time and time again."

"You hit it on the button, but it's never going to change."

"I wouldn't say never baby, people just need a reason to change."

"It's funny that you say that because we talked about that to some degree yesterday. The girl's mom name is Jasmine. Well anyway, she was telling me that I needed to be a spokesperson for women who were victims of domestic violence or sexual abuse because of how I handled the situation with her daughter."

"You're talking about the woman that was at the door with you yesterday."

"Yes. Melanie wouldn't talk to her mother or Jess, but it didn't take much for me to break the ice. I held her and made her feel comfortable and she responded well to that. I was just loving and honest with her, but she'll continue to be a work in progress."

"You can't turn your back on her and I personally believe you would make an excellent spokesperson. Do what needs to be done baby."

"Melissa and the girls pretty much said the same thing to me."

"Okay, so what's the problem? I can take care of the girls, or you know my mom don't mind taking them rascals off our hands. In fact, I know she'd love to."

"I don't even know where to start at. I can't just go around knocking on folks doors and ask if anyone who lives there is a victim of domestic violence or sexual abuse."

"Of course not silly; we can put together an organization for you, and you can set appointments on when you speak and where you'll speak."

"What if I needed a mentor or a group of people to mentor them young guys that's growing up in those unstable households, can I count on you?"

"Of course you can. I fully support you with whatever you decide to do."

"Thank you baby. It's time for me to have that talk with the ladies."

"Do what you have to do and let me know what you need from me."

Jessica was the first one that I called. I informed her that she would have to be a major player, and then I pitched the idea of the Sisterhood forming an organization that would target domestic violence, sexual abuse and troubled youths. I also shared with her how I wanted to open up Boy's and Girl's clubs.

"That's a great idea Key. You need to call and get everybody together. Make sure you let them know your plans too."

I took her advice and began to put things in motion. A few of the girls had other obligations which prevented us from getting together ASAP, so we all agreed to meet up in a few weeks. That was cool. It gave me more than enough time to have everything in place. Since that was all taken care of I shifted all my attention to Melanie. I stopped by to see her like I promised, but instead of sitting around in the house, me, Jess, Melanie and my two daughters went to the movies. Melanie was much more talkative than she was the day before. I guess that's because she was comfortable with me and she knew I'd protect her.

"She's back to her normal self Key," Jessica shared. "I got to their house a few hours before you came and she was full of life asking when you were coming. We don't know how we'll ever be able to repay you for making that possible. I guess I can start off by saying thanks and that I love you. I speak for Jasmine and Melanie too."

"Aw, thank you Jess, but you don't owe me anything. We're sisters and that's what we're supposed to do. Always be there for each other."

After the movies we kicked it at Dave & Buster's, where the girls played games for a while. I enjoyed watching them have fun and wondered what life would've been like when I was their age, had my mother not used drugs and alcohol. I also wondered about what I would be doing in life had that been the case. I went in a daze with all types of thoughts running through my head.

"Hey you."

"What! You scared the hell out of me!" I snapped.

"I didn't mean to, I was just speaking."

"I'm afraid I don't know you."

"You shut me down before you got a chance to."

"Excuse me!"

"Years ago in the club you turned me down with no hesitation. You wouldn't dance with me, accept a drink from me, no nothing."

"What makes you think things will be any different now," I asked, showing off my wedding ring.

"I just couldn't resist stopping by and saying hello. Congratulations though."

"Thank you."

As he was walking away, Bria was running up to me. She jumped in my lap, looked me in the eyes and gave me a kiss. I hugged her tight and gave her a kiss of my own, followed by another hug.

"I love you mommy."

"I love you too baby."

"I'm hungry mommy."

"Okay, let's go get everybody else so we can go eat."

"Ok mommy."

They wanted to go eat at Chucky Cheese, so we rode to the one in Monroeville. Bria really was hungry. She was gobbling pizza down like there was no tomorrow. Watching the girls stuff themselves reminded me of the time when me, Janet and Robin went to Ponderosa with Momma Sue and Mr. Damon.

We ate so much that we couldn't move, and now as I watched them, I couldn't stop laughing.

We found something different to do every single day for two weeks. Melanie had gotten so attached to us that she would call on her own and talk for long periods of time. Jasmine asked me to be Melanie's Godmother, which opened the door for her to spend the night with us from time to time. She loved my' baby's as if they were actually her sisters. They were the future of the Sisterhood.

The time had finally come for us to meet up. All I had was ideas, nothing planned like I expected to. I was having so much fun with Melanie and my daughters that I let time slip by me. With all of us working together though, I was certain all the plans would be in place soon.

"Well ladies, the purpose of us all getting together is because I want to become active in targeting females who went through domestic violence, victims of sexual abuse, and troubled youths. I want to open up Boy's and Girl's clubs throughout the city. With that we could have after school programs where we would not just help them with their homework, but make sure they can comprehend all the work they do. I also want them to have access to different games, computers, and since we're all excellent dancers, they could learn different dance routines. We can put together a cheerleading squad."

"Girl I haven't done any cheerleading routines in years," Dannielle told me.

"You found a way to shake all that ass before. I'm sure you'll still be able to manage."

"I'm not going there with you," she said, trying to hold back from laughing.

"Thank you Ma."

"We can put together a non-profit organization and have people donate money to us for it. I believe a lot of people in the higher ups would be supportive of what we're planning," Janet shared.

"What about a name?" Robin asked.

"It has to be something that relates to male and females in the struggle," Dannielle elaborated.

"What about BBNB Inc?" Melissa asked.

"What does that stand for?" Robin asked.

"Battered But Not Broken Incorporated," Melissa revealed.

"I like that. The word battered represents the pain," Robin added.

"Lis, you know you'll have to be one of the main voices in this," I told her.

"Why doesn't that come as a surprise to me? I've been a voice since the first day you met me. It would be selfish of me to stop now. I'm in it for the long haul."

"I know, I know Lis. I just wanted to put that out there mainly because I needed to hear you say it. I can't lie to any of y'all though, I'm afraid to fail."

"Key, have you ever heard of a saying about your thoughts becoming your actions?"

"Yeah, Momma Sue used to always tell us to be careful about what we put in the Universe, because we could speak it into existence."

"You're doing exactly what she told you not to do."

"I know. It's just that my life is perfect for me right now and I'm afraid to step outside of my comfort zone."

"Keya listen to me and listen carefully," Melissa said with a straight face. "We are living testimonies and females from the ages of ten to fifty will gather around us to listen for words they can cling to. As we move forward with this, always remember that a little hope is all faith needs."

"You always know what to say. That's why I love you and the rest of my sisters so much."

CHAPTER 8

After getting our name trademarked, we made some recordings of our lectures and sent them to middle schools, high schools, colleges, and anywhere else we could reach a group of people so that our voices could be heard. All of us had a story to tell from growing up without a mother or father, having parents hooked on drugs, over-protective parents, or our experiences of being raped and beaten. We got great feedback, and a few high schools invited us to do our lectures in person. Being that most of us in the sisterhood went to Schenley High, it felt rewarding having that be the first ever place we spoke. It was a great experience and I honestly felt that we all did a great job. As in all situations, there were people with mixed emotions. Some giggled, others cried, and most of them just stared in disbelief. When the lecture was over, we gave them the opportunity to ask questions.

"You in the back row with the pink shirt on, what's your question?" I asked her.

"My name is Marva and my question is for Janet. Did not having your father in your life make you feel vulnerable? Did it make you crave for love and affection outside of your home?"

"That's a good question Marva. I guess I can say that I did have those cravings in the beginning when I was younger. Constantly seeing other kids with their dads, and always hearing them talk about them had me wondering what that feeling was like. I didn't have to search far though. It was a family environment over my best friends Keya and Robin's house," Janet spoke honestly. "Next question."

"Yeah my name is Jerome and my question is for Melissa with her fine self."

Everybody chuckled after the comment he made, then the room immediately got quiet when Melissa walked to the front of the room.

"And what's your question Jerome?"

"It's not that often that you hear about a boyfriend raping his girlfriend. I can only imagine how that devastated you mentally, emotionally and physically. Did you have major trust issues with people, and if so, how long did it take for you to recover in all those aspects?"

"Wow, you're an intelligent charmer."

The class erupted in laughter at Melissa's humor, so she waited until it died down to answer Jerome's question.

"To answer your questions, I was most definitely devastated. I got violated by someone I had feelings for. The physical aspect of it wasn't as bad for me as it was mentally and emotionally. It took a long time for me to fully understand why he did that to me, because we would've eventually gotten to that point. I had trust issues that I thought I'd possess forever, but by my mother being a spiritual woman, my faith in God helped me get through. As far as the recovery thing; you can never fully recover from something like that. It's a day to day, lifetime process. I hope I answered your question clearly."

"Yes you did. Thank you."

"I have a question for Jessica," a girl named Sally sitting in the middle of the classroom spoke.

"Okay, and what is your question?" Jessica asked.

"I listened to you carefully about the experience you went through. Looking back on your situation, what warning signs would you advise people to watch out for?"

"That's an excellent question Sally. I would advise people to be on alert when there's excessive touching. My uncle was a great role model in the beginning, but my body began to develop around the time his wife left him, and I guess I can go as far as saying that situation mentally and emotionally messed him up, and he used me to fill that void. I was partly the blame for not confiding in my mother. But everyone must take into consideration that by not reaching out for help in those type of situations, it could come back to haunt the next person."

"Thank you Jessica."

"You're very welcome."

"I have a question."

"Okay and what's your name and question?" Jessica asked.

"My name is June and I never knew my father. Growing up my mom did everything she could to make sure I had the best, but to this day I still carry around that bitterness for not having my dad in my life. What can y'all do for people in my situation, besides from sharing y'all stories?"

"I got this one," Robin told us. "We'll have something like a big brother program, where you'll have mentors that'll spend time with you and do things to replenish that fatherly love that's missing. On top of that, we're in the process of opening up Boy's & Girl's clubs in different communities. Our purpose will be to help tutor students that may have a little trouble with their school work, give others an opportunity to do their homework, and have a place to play and enjoy themselves afterwards if they like. We'll also have basketball leagues against other Boy's & Girl's clubs. There'll be teams for both the boys and girls, with cheerleaders. We'll also have an apprenticeship program so everyone can learn different trades, and we're trying to organize a program that'll provide all the members with summer jobs. Trust me June, we have everyone's best interest at heart. It might not be of the same magnitude, but all of us have experienced hardship to some degree. We just hope and pray that the people, or should I say young adults, will take advantage of what we're offering."

"Who could refuse all of that?" June spoke.

"You'll be surprised," Robin added. "For the most part people want all the pleasures in life handed to them on a silver platter. We'll see what happens though."

That concluded our lecture. We encouraged everyone to be a voice of reasoning when necessary, because everyone had an influence on someone, then I closed out.

"Hello everyone, my name is Keya and I just want to say a few things. Our business cards are being passed around, and on them you'll see our office phone number, along with a twenty-four hour contact number. Please don't hesitate to call any of those numbers if it's a crisis, or you just need someone to talk to. I have one more thing to say. It's very, very important to be a voice of reasoning instead of being one of those people that adds fuel to fires. What I'm saying fits our motto. To the world you might just be one person, but to one person you might be the world. I thank you all for your time, and I encourage everyone to pick up the phone and give us a call if need be. We're all very good listeners if given a chance."

All the ladies were very happy about how things turned out. The students had great questions and we gave them great, truthful answers. My doubts that I had were gone, and I was more motivated than ever to get started with our projects. Robin had surprised us with the ideas she pitched to the students, and Mya made sure she recorded every word just in case Robin was freestyling.

Ty found us a fairly large building in downtown Pittsburgh, located near Grant Street. All fourteen of us had our own office and everyone was in charge of different branches of our corporation. Mike and Mont were in charge of finding the buildings all over the city that we could have our clubs at, but the locations were the problem.

"Baby, we found a lot of buildings at nice prices, but I don't like where they're located at. For an example, there's one we found in Manchester and Perrysville. Both of them are located in high crime areas. It's the same for Homewood, the Hill District, and all over the city," Mike rambled on.

"You know what though Mike, they might be the best locations. We want to reach out to the troubled youths, who most of them have dropped out of school. The streets are their family now and our goal is to change that."

"You know it's not going to be easy. The majority of them will probably resist. We have to prepare ourselves for the negativity and possible violence."

"Me and the rest of the ladies are all in. We refuse to allow them to push us away. I believe in my heart that we'll be able to reach out and grow on them."

"I'm with you one hundred percent Key. I told you that when I put the ring on your finger."

"Thank you baby. I love you so much."

"I love you too."

Mike was able to put together a deal that got us the buildings we needed in Homewood, the Hill District, Manchester, Perrysville, Beltzoover, Sheridan, Larimer, Braddock, Duquesne, Aliquippa, St. Clair Village and Hazelwood. He got us twelve buildings in all, but they needed a major face lift. It would take several months for the remodeling, nevertheless; we were all excited that our plans were moving along.

We received a surprise phone call from the Mayor commending us on the things we've been doing in the community, and he wanted us to speak at the Convention Center about the experiences we went through and how we endured it all. He also wanted the rest of the world to know about our plans to protect our youth from the experiences we went through. We accepted his offer and began to prepare because we only had a week to do so. Three days before the event I got a phone call.

"Since when have I started being the last to know about things? Especially major things?"

"I'm sorry, I been so-."

"That's the same exact thing Robin tried to say to me when I called her. Stop being so sorry all the time, I'm just glad that you finally decided to do something with yourself and you managed to bring all your lazy sisters along with you. Baby if there's anything y'all need from me, please don't hesitate to call me. Oh by the way, trust and believe that I'll be there for the big day. Damon told me to tell you that he loves you and that he's proud of you. You're doing the right thing baby. There's people out there that don't have the strength and courage you have.
People may need to draw strength from you."

"Thanks mom, your love and support means the world to me."

"Okay, give my babies a hug and kiss for me, and tell them grandma loves them."

"I'll make sure they call you later and tell you goodnight."

To my surprise, I didn't get the ear beating that I expected from Momma Sue. The words she shared gave me even more confidence. I was finally starting to believe this is what I was supposed to be doing. In order to help and be appreciated, people had to know what I went through and how I overcame everything, and was still blessed with the life I always wanted.

The day before our big event I called Momma Sue to get her opinion on a few things. She told me to call if I needed her, so I was cashing in on that.

"What's wrong baby?"

"What makes you think there's something wrong with me?"

"Girl I know you better than you know yourself."

"That's deep," I told her. "Mom I'm starting to get cold feet."

"That's natural. Everyone goes through that baby."

"Are you sure?"

"Would I lie to you?"

"Of course not. You'll be here tomorrow right?"

"I wouldn't miss it for nothing in the world baby. Don't talk crazy."

That conversation helped me calm my nerves a little bit. I slept good that night, but when I woke up in the morning I had cold feet, jitters, butterflies, or whatever you want to call it. Something had to give, it was officially showtime.

Janet took the honors of starting the show off after the Mayor got everyone in their seats and introduced our organization. He spoke a little about our constant effort to help those in the community, then gave us the stage. All the ladies in the sisterhood spoke to some degree.

"Hello everyone, my name is Janet Howard and I'm a representative for the BBNB Inc. ... Our purpose here tonight is to share the stories of our trials and tribulations, then talk about how we overcame it all and what we're doing to help our youth. I grew up without my father in my life, and in the beginning it affected me mentally to the point where I couldn't focus on or comprehend none of my school work. I failed in the third grade, but my mom paid for a tutor and I eventually caught back up. The hardest part of not having a father was when I watched or heard the other kids talking about how their fathers took them to do fun things. I so desperately craved for that fatherly love and affection. I'm just thankful that I didn't search all the wrong places for it. I used the love from my close friends and family to get through those hard times. Everyone's not as fortunate as I was. That's why we formed this organization and we encourage all of you to support us with our movement. Thank you, enjoy the rest of the evening."

Jessica was up next to speak in front of the large crowd. I was so nervous for her, so I made it my business to keep my distance because I didn't want her to see me shaking uncontrollably and make her nervous.

"Hello everyone, my name is Jessica Adams. Life started off rough for me, I never had my father in my life. My mom did a great job of filling that void, but there was nothing she could do to stop people from calling me muts or wanna be black girl. Being that I'm bi-racial, I socialized with the whites and blacks, but there were some people that didn't like the idea of me communicating with both. It eventually got old though and things became normal in my life. That was until my father's brother started coming around. In the beginning him and his wife embraced me as if I were their own. Everything was great until they separated. He was still the sweet, caring uncle, just more hands on. One day he gently grabbed me by the back of my neck and started kissing me, It was confusing to me not just because he was my uncle, I was a freshman in high school and I had never been kissed or touched before. I was so confused, I kept it to myself. On the days that I went to school from his house, he'd walk in the bathroom on me and wash me up. As time went on he eventually started touching me in my private parts, then the molesting started heavily. I was afraid to tell my mother about what was going on, so I stopped going over his house altogether. I came home one day from school and my uncle was there waiting on me. My mother wasn't home yet and I was terrified. After barking at me for avoiding him, he snatched me up and took me to my room. He aggressively ripped my clothes off and made me lay on my stomach. He forced himself inside me and I screamed my lungs out. Surprisingly my mother ran through my bedroom door and was horrified by what she saw. She ran to get her gun, but he managed to escape before she came back. He eventually got arrested and charged. When I had to testify and relive those horrible moments I ended up in a mental hospital for almost two years. By the grace of God I was able to bounce back. Now reaching out to people and helping is very important to me. It could be someone close to one of you here tonight that's going through what I went through, or inflicting the pain. The BBNB Inc. could use all the sponsors and support that we can get. I humbly ask each of you here tonight for your help in saving our youth. Thank you all, I hope you enjoy the rest of the evening."

Jessica did an excellent job and the crowd was very receptive to her. She didn't appear to be nervous at all and I envied her for having so much courage, because I was a nervous wreck. Melissa was called to the stage next, so I watched from afar to see how she responded.

"Good evening ladies and gentleman, my name is Melissa Hamilton and I'm a victim of domestic violence and sexual abuse. When I was in middle school my boyfriend that I was in love with constantly pressured me to have sex with him. When I told him no time after time he got fed up and decided to take what he wanted. He convinced me to stop at his house as he was walking me home from school, and that's where the rape took place. I don't want to dive into all the details, but when he finished sexually assaulting me; he beat me up and spit in my face. I lost every ounce of self-esteem that I had. I was hurt and confused, plus it took me a long time to feel comfortable around anyone other than family. My mother was my rock and somehow she convinced me that he was the one who was actually suffering and that I was hurting for him. As we began to get deeper into the bible I started to believe and the internal healing began. I never forgot the fact that I had been violated, but that experience made me stronger. There's an old saying that says: What don't kill you only makes you stronger. That true statement is why I'm standing before you today, with hopes that we'll all unite and take a stand against domestic violence and sexual abuse. We also need to reach out and help our youth and take them back from the streets. Thank you very much and God bless you all."

    I was the next person to speak and Robin was closing it out. The only problem was that I was too afraid to step on the stage because my nerves were uncontrollable. My husband was in attendance showing his support, but at this particular time I needed Momma Sue. Melissa and Robin gave me a nod to assure me everything was okay, yet and still, I wasn't feeling so confident. As Janet took the honors to introduce me, I paced back and forth trying to get or find that push I needed to get through this. I tensed up when I felt a hand touch my shoulder.

    "I'm here baby, you can do it," Momma Sue told me.

I took a deep breath, turned around and looked at her, then gave her a confident smile. I walked on that stage with my head held high and surveyed the crowd. I continued to stare into the crowd until they came to a complete silence.

"Hello, my name is Keya Gibson-Carson and I was a victim of domestic violence and sexual abuse twice. Some of you amongst us this evening may know me and most of you don't. What's important is that we are all people of the same struggle. Our common goal here tonight is to overcome the mental, emotional and physical damage that we have suffered and are still suffering. We have to somehow stop it from trickling down to our youth. When I was thirteen years of age my biological mother pawned me off to one of her drug addict friends and I was raped. I have never felt so cheap and violated in my life and had it not been for the woman that I'll always consider as my real mother, I would've continuously gotten violated and beaten by my mother. Thank you Momma Sue, I love you so much. She rescued me from those horrible moments in my life. The woman that gave birth to me and the man she accepted money from and allowed to violate me went to jail, but they never made it out of there alive."

"There was another time when I was in college and my ex-boyfriend who was a woman beater, decided to get revenge on me for breaking up with him. I couldn't stay in a relationship with a man that abused drugs, then abused me when he needed someone to hit on. To this day I still don't know how he found out where I lived, but he brought a friend with him, who helped force his way in and rape me. They both had on mask, but I knew who he was from the birth mark on his thigh. I was already furious that he took delight in beating on me, so when the opportunity presented itself I put him through tremendous pain. That's how the police were able to arrest and prosecute both men. The damage was already done though. For so long the love in me was dead. My soul was dead and I tried to take my own life. I ended up in a mental hospital where I met Jessica and some of the other ladies that spoke tonight. I was at the point of no return. It was pretty much impossible for me to replenish what was missing inside of me. As time went on, throughout all the pain that I endured, I learned that when we live the way God intended for us to, everything good comes to us. It might not come in the exact form or fashion that we pray for, but our spirits are full of joy. He never feeds us to the point where we're full. The reason being is because once the hunger is gone, the ability to change and our desires are gone. As I stand here before you in my true essence of a woman, I can tell you with truth and conviction; that when love is real and you learn the art of loving yourself; you'll see firsthand that love's not supposed to hurt. Take it from someone who has been a recipient of real love. I never thought that I'd find happiness after all the misery I consumed, but I've been blessed with a strong, loving, caring and understanding husband, along with two daughters. The only way to get out of the state of mind and existence we're in is to embrace change. It can't hurt, look what change has done for me and my associates. The biggest challenge in life is getting out of old habits to try something new. Change is good and as a unit it can be great."

"On the flipside to what I said to you earlier ladies and gentleman, we as women, nurturers of the lives that are brought into this world, must also step up and take some of the blame for the problems with our youth. A lot of us are so desperate to seek instant gratification that we become sexually active with men that just prey on our weakness. When we pop up pregnant, most of those men leave us alone to raise these children. It's hard for the average women to raise a male alone and as those children begin to grow and understand things, they consume bitterness and hatred in their hearts. Most of them eventually turn to the streets, where the drug lords are their fathers, the crime rate is higher in our communities and we're losing a large amount of the male population to the prison systems. Let's make this a better environment for our youth to grow up in and appreciate by coming together and making that possible. Let's be more active at our children's schools, by being voices at the meetings and things of that nature."

"Before I finish up my speech I have a poem that I want to share with everyone. I wrote it myself and the name of the poem is called, "He Chose Me."

He Chose Me

I was horribly sacrificed as a child and I didn't have a clue as to why my life took those turn of events.

My mom tried to justify her inexcusable actions by telling me that it was the only way to pay the rent.

Feeling worthless and cheap, the love of my new family helped me move forward and put behind me my dreadful past.

And then the day that I met Mr. Mike Carson, I honestly felt like my life was finally perfect at last.

But sometimes love can make you insecure and I lost the love of my life because fools do foolish things.

When we act off impulses and jump into things or situations head first, we never see the drama that it brings.

I entered another relationship and after months of being beaten and tormented, I sat and asked myself why.

He couldn't take me parting ways, so he decided to rape me, beat me, then he left me there to die.

I didn't want to go on with life, my suicide attempts failed, but then I received a message from the man above.

His message was clear, he said Keya stand up and fight, share your testimony, and provide those that need you with love.

He re-connected me with the man of my dreams, along with two beautiful daughters to complete the deal.

He also put us ladies together to form the BBNB Inc. to present to you, to show me that his message was real.

He also told me that he would never put me in any situation I couldn't handle, and that some sacrifices just had to be.

He said he needed a voice to reach out to people and save lives, that's why...

He Chose Me!!

"Thank you ladies and gentleman."

The crowd applauded for what seemed to be hours and all the speakers that spoke thus far walked back on stage to soak it all in. The Mayor stood up while he clapped, encouraging the rest of the crowd to do the same. The feeling felt so good and I was so proud of all my sisters. We set out to do something collectively and received a much bigger praise and acknowledgements than we ever anticipated. When

LOVE'S NOT SUPPOSED TO HURT

the crowd began to calm down, I grabbed the microphone again.

"Excuse me ladies and gentleman. We have one more speaker left. Robin Wallace will conclude things tonight by filling everyone in on our plans and where we are with those plans so far. With that being said, I present to you, Ms. Robin Wallace."

"Hello ladies and gents, as you already know, my name is Robin Wallace. I'm here to discuss with you how the BBNB Inc. came to life and our purpose. The BBNB Inc. was assembled because we're a sisterhood that's been through our share of hardship, happiness and disagreements. We felt like we have a lot to offer to society, mainly our youth. People gain knowledge through experience, which we all have done, but to know something and not share it is like not knowing at all. We don't want to make that mistake, so here we are at the forefront."

"Our plans are to open up Boy's and Girl's clubs throughout the city. We have buildings located in Manchester and Perrysville on the Northside, in Braddock and Homewood on the Eastside. We have one location on the Westside, which is Sheridan. On the Southside we have Beltzoover and St. Clair Village locations, and last Aliquippa in Beaver County. With these clubs, we plan to help tutor students that need help, have a place for them to do their homework, then have a little fun afterwards. Since all twelve locations will be ran by the BBNB Inc., we're working out the details to have traveling basketball leagues for the boys and girls. For the girls that don't play basketball, they'll have an opportunity to be a cheerleader for their respective team. We also have plans to provide apprenticeship programs so that everyone can learn different trades. We're hoping this will draw the young men out there away from the streets. Last but not least, with the help of the community leaders, we're trying to organize a program that'll provide all members with summer jobs. All of our plans are designed with everyone's best interest at heart. If we have any type of say so, we want to prevent the young people of the world from dealing with the hardships we endured. We just hope and pray that the support is there to help solidify our goals. We really appreciate all of you for coming out and joining us tonight. The number of people in attendance shows me that a lot of us really do care about our precious community. Hopefully this is one of many meetings we'll have. Goodnight ladies and gents, and God bless you all."

The Mayor and the rest of the people in attendance were blown away with how organized we were and the manner in which we presented ourselves. Over a hundred people handed us business cards telling us how much they would love doing business with us.

The after party got us more praise from those we didn't get an opportunity to speak to at the Convention Center. When the evening was over with, we had at least four hundred business cards. We were so proud of ourselves, and we had the right to feel that way.

"I'm proud of you," Mike told me when we got home that night.

"Thank you. Hearing that from you means a whole lot to me."

"The poem was touching too. It took all the willpower that I had not to cry. I actually saw a few people around me shed a tear though. I'm glad you and the girls made this decision."

"I am too; especially now that my speech is over. Baby I was so nervous in the beginning that I literally shook like I was standing outside with no coat on in below zero weather. Momma Sue must've sensed something, because she came and comforted me."

"Being nervous is a natural thing baby. I always had butterflies before each game, but once the game got started I calmed down. It won't be the last time you feel nervous, but you'll be okay like you were today."

"You have so much confidence in me."

"After it was all over everyone in attendance was confident in you too."

"Thank you baby."

Mike drifted off to sleep but my adrenaline was still going and I couldn't sleep. I turned the television on, but after surfing through the channels and finding nothing I picked up a book. The book was titled Hard Times, by an author named Tommy Shorter. I turned on my reading lamp, fluffed my pillows and began to read.

HARD TIME

As I sit and await the judge's ruling, my mind drifts back to the good ole days when I was in college, before I made a foolish decision to dive head first into the drug game to rescue my family from poverty. I was riding on a full scholarship at the University of Penn State for football. I had a promising career playing wide receiver with my six foot, four inch frame, up until the day my mother and two sisters got evicted for not being able to pay the rent. I was pissed off, embarrassed, you name it. Quite naturally, I was desperate to help my family out, so I went to my friend's uncle who was a big time drug dealer and I asked him for some help until I entered the NFL draft, which I was projected to be a first round pick. The only problem was that I still had a whole college season to play first. I asked him to loan me fifty thousand dollars, which I knew was nothing to him and I promised to pay him back two hundred thousand. Although what I was doing was against the law and violated NCAA rules, I couldn't allow my mother and sisters to be cramped up in a three bedroom apartment with my aunt and her four children. My father was only good at neglecting his responsibilities, so I was their only hope. I didn't tell my mother what I was up to though, because she would never approve. Stephen, my friend's uncle that I sought the loan from, had a different plan that he said would generate even more money for me if I played my cards right. He wanted me to sell OxyContin to the college students and he guaranteed me that I'd make enough money to do whatever I dreamed of doing. He gave me fifty of them to pass out to different people and before I knew it, I had people coming at me from all angles. I was already a popular guy on campus, but selling drugs enhanced my popularity to a level beyond my wildest dreams. In four months I was able to buy my mother and two sisters a nice house, plus I had a rack of money left for myself. Right then and there I was supposed to quit, especially when I started carrying an unlicensed gun around, but the addiction I inherited overwhelmed me. Somewhere along the line I picked up an enemy or two, and one of those jealous sons of bitches dropped a dime on me. When the school security and local police raided my room they found a loaded .38 special, a thousand OxyContin's, and close to ten thousand dollars. I couldn't believe this was happening to me. To make a long story short, I got kicked out of school, the feds picked up my case, and Stephen disappeared off the face of the earth. The press was all over it, constantly writing articles about another prominent black athlete throwing away a dream for the life of crime. I still had an opportunity to live out my dream of playing professional football, but the only way that could happen was if I snitched on Stephen or any other big named dealer, which was not an option for me. I told myself that I'd rather die before I put my family in danger, so I went to trial instead of taking the deal for a hundred and fifty-one months. Even though I never had a record, my lawyer told me that was the best deal available, so I decided to fight and lost.

Judge Bonnie Jameson looked me in my eyes and told me all the reasons why she didn't want to sentence me in her courtroom before she sentenced me to two hundred and thirty five months. I couldn't believe what I heard. I was having trouble breathing and my vision was blurry. I had some choice words for Judge Jameson, but I kept them to myself and was quietly escorted out the courtroom.

I marked the page I stopped on and put the book down. It hurt me to my heart to see people throw away their lives for some nice clothes, cars and women that only hung around because things were good, but the moment things went sour they ran to the next one. The character that I was reading about reminded me of a guy named Ernie that I went to school with. He was the star quarterback when Mike graduated from high school, but Mike tried to talk some sense into Ernie, which did no good. With him being only sixteen years old riding around in a Lexus coupe, there wasn't nothing anyone could tell him. Now as he sits in state prison at Albion with a fifteen year sentence, he wishes that he would've taken the advice we all tried to give him. He was a friend of ours, so me and Mike send him money every month, and we write as much as we can. It's crazy how life goes though. Ernie's now into church real deep and at the top of every letter he sends it says, wealth gained dishonestly will diminish, but he who gathers it through labor will increase. Proverbs 13:11 was his favorite scripture, because it kept him grounded. As my eyes began to get heavy I turned off the lights and was sound asleep shortly afterwards.

The next morning Momma Sue stopped by our house with Mr. Damon to see us before they left to go back home. It was funny looking at Momma Sue who was always full of life, because instead of aging over the years, she still looked young and was in excellent shape.

"Hi Mike," Momma Sue greeted him, so full of energy when she walked through the door. "Where's Keya and my girls at?"

"They're all upstairs."

"Okay, well I'm going upstairs while you guys talk about them sports."

"Yeah we need that. It's a whole lot of sports to talk about."

"Karen and Bria, grandma's here!"

"Hi grandma!" Bria hollered as she ran out to greet her.

"Where's Karen at?"

"In the room getting her hair done."

"Come on, let's go see her."

"Hi grandma!" Karen shouted as they entered the room.

. "Hello to you cutey. And who are you?" Momma Sue asked the girl doing Karen's hair.

"My name is Melanie."

"It's good to meet you Melanie. Do you think you can do my hair like that?"

"Yes Ma'am."

"Ool, you're a polite little something ain't you?"

"I try to be," Melanie said, cracking a little smile.

"I'll be back to check on y'all, I have to go talk to mommy."

"Okay grandma," Bria said, running to give Momma Sue a hug and kiss.

"I love my little cutey pie," Momma Sue told her.

She walked in my room only to find me sound asleep. All the events from the night before, then staying up and reading took its toll on me. I really wanted to sleep the whole day away but Momma Sue had other plans though. She kissed me on my cheek and rubbed my shoulder gently.

"Hey sleepy head," she said, as I opened my eyes. "You need to go take care of that tongue before we start talking," she continued.

I got up, stretched, and then went to the bathroom to get myself together. I felt drained, so I took me a quick shower, brushed my teeth, then went back to my bedroom where Momma Sue was still waiting.

"You look much better. Come here and let me smell your breath."

"No, that's the stuff I do to my kids mom. I'm not a kid anymore."

"You and Robin will always be my babies, don't ever forget that."

"I know, but it's a big difference now, we're grown. There's just some things we grow out of."

"That's not one of them, next conversation. All of you did a great job yesterday and I wanted to personally come tell you how proud I am since we really didn't get to talk last night. I constantly surveyed the crowd and I noticed that everyone was zoned in listening to the speeches."

"I noticed that too. We had a couple hundred people give us their business cards. All of them said they would love to invest and be a part of our movement, so it feels good to accomplish something."

"I always believed in y'all. The key is to keep pushing no matter how hard it gets. Those weren't ordinary people out in the audience last night. They were key figure heads in the city. With the Mayor backing this thing too, it's a win, win situation."

"I know. When I stop and think about everything, I still can't believe it's real. I just keep looking to wake up to all of this being a dream.

"It started out as a dream. You just have to take into consideration dreams come true. Now all you have to do is ride the wave and complete the mission."

"How do you think those kids heavy in the streets will react to the programs we're setting up in their neighborhoods?"

"What do you mean?"

"Do you think they'll join what we're trying to do, rebel against us or just forget about us altogether?"

"You know, that's the one thing that frustrates me. You worry too much about the things you can't control, instead of just trying to focus on what you're trying to accomplish. What difference does it make if nobody comes, just do your part. When you put your all into something, you never have to live with regrets. So for future reference, save the silly questions."

"You're right. It's just that I'm investing my heart and soul into this and I don't want to fail. Momma Sue this is like my third child and I don't want anything to happen to it. I know you can understand where I'm coming from."

"Absolutely. I'm glad that you used that terminology. How far will you go to protect your children?"

"There are no limitations. I'll do whatever it takes."

"My point exactly. Now do whatever it takes to make things work because there's no such thing as failure with us. The only time you truly fail is when you don't even try. From now on I don't want to hear that word, you understand me?"

"Yes I understand."

"Good, I have to get back in the other room and spend a little time with my girls. I'll see you downstairs."

I took my time getting dressed because I spent a lot of time in a daze thinking about my fear of failing and what Momma Sue said to me. She was right, we had powerful people backing us and I needed to focus all my energy and attention on the task at hand. In regards to people joining, along with all the other silly questions I asked, we'll just be there to provide for the people who do show up and deal with any problem that comes our way. Mike and his boys were in charge of the security, so some of the money from the contributions would pay for that and everything else we needed. As I thought further into it I had to laugh because it was silly of me to ever think this would fail. I jumped up, got myself dressed and joined the rest of the family downstairs.

CHAPTER 9

No matter how great things appeared to be for our organization, there was still doubt or fear inside of me that something would go wrong. During my life experiences, when things seemed to be going well for me a dark cloud would emerge and bring misery into my world. My belief is that karma works in mysterious ways and that it doesn't always target a particular person. Me and my brothers could've possibly inherited the karma from our mother or our poor excuse for fathers. All my doubts and fears quickly diminished when Mike told us the renovation on the buildings for the Boy's and Girl's clubs were practically done. A sigh of relief came down on me and the energy in the office shifted drastically. We all were overwhelmed with excitement. We had a vision, and to actually see it come to life was unexplainable. After we all settled down a little bit, Robin called the Mayor to share the good news, knowing he would relay it to the rest of our associates.

"Hello Mr. Mayor, this is Robin from the BBNB Inc."

"Yes, how are you doing today Robin?"

"I'm fine; I just called to share some news with you."

"You have my undivided attention."

"The renovations on the buildings are almost done and we'll be able to have things up and running soon."

"That's great news. I feel blessed seeing everything come into fruition. I'll relay the message to the others and hopefully we'll be able to take a tour soon."

"That won't be a problem Sir. As soon as you find free time in your busy schedule we'll make it happen."

"Give me about a week or so. That'll give all of us enough time to free up our schedules."

"No problem."

The Mayor and the others were free the following week. During our walk through of the building in Homewood, Robin made it perfectly clear to everyone that all opinions mattered and any input that was beneficial to our projects would be appreciated. None of our guest had anything to add at that particular time, but we were surely hoping and looking forward to listening and learning from all of them. They knew exactly what was going on in our society from a statistical standpoint and what it would take to fix things.

About three weeks after our tour, I got a call from the City Councilman. He confided in me how pleased he was of our dedication to reach out to and help those in need. He also had a very interesting suggestion that he shared with me, but I invited him to stop by our office so he could address it with everyone. I set up a meeting that suited his crazy schedule and we got down to business.

"Ladies, I called this meeting because the City Councilman, Mr. David Berkley brought something to my attention. I asked him if he could stop in and share that same news with everyone. So with that being said, the floor is yours Mr. Berkley."

"Thank you Keya, and I really wish you would call me Dave," he said cracking a slight smile. "Well ladies, I came here today to present the idea that my colleagues and I came up with, for the BBNB Inc. to get licensed to run foster homes along with the rest of your plans. We've done our thorough research and we found that Melissa has the credentials to make things happen. Please continue to hear me out ladies before you object. As we speak, there are thousands of homeless people running around because they have no place to go, or no one to turn to. The streets become their parents, where they become addicts, drug dealers, prostitutes, thieves, you name it. I hear so often that one person can't change the world, but if we devote our time and energy into reaching out to one or two at a time, the numbers will soon multiply. Accepting this proposal would be a great service to our community and you'll be pretty much killing two birds with one stone."

"And how is that?" Jessica asked.

"We can get access to a building that'll house up to six hundred people, plus it has an indoor gym that can be used for the basketball league you have planned. You'll receive grants that will provide food and clothing for everyone. If this project is a success, which I know it will be; we'll be able to open up more foster homes throughout the city."

"Why us?" Melissa asked. "There are plenty of organizations already established that could take on this task. I know at least three of them off the top of my head."

"That's a great question. The reason why we're targeting your organization is because of the passion each of you show when it comes to helping others and giving back to the community. My colleagues and I have nothing but great things to say about the BBNB Inc. and society could use some fresh blood out there. Do know that if your organization agrees to help, there will be more than enough money donated, and from grants to hire a highly qualified staff. We just need someone to oversee things and help the needy, which fits you. This project can be an extension to what you already have going on. Basically ladies, you have a lot of powerful people behind you that's willing to contribute to anything you bring to the table. We're not looking for an immediate answer, but I ask you to please process all the information that I've given to you. I speak for everyone when I say that we truly hope we can consolidate our plans and work hard towards bettering our precious community."

"We truly appreciate you for stopping by Dave. You can look forward to hearing from us soon," I told him.

As soon as he left we began to converse amongst each other. We all agreed when forming our organization, that we wouldn't make quick decisions and that all decisions would be made collectively. We went to the round table and started our process.

"It sounds like a great idea," Janet spoke. "The only problem that I see is us taking on different challenges at one time. I say let's breathe life into our baby first, then take on other challenges."

"You have a valid point, but think about this scenario Jan," Melissa spoke.

"The foster home is a great opportunity to get kids off the streets and to use our project as an outlet for education, recreation or whatever else they can get out of it. I believe we can pull it off, especially with us being able to hire extra staff."

"I believe we can pull it off," Kelly joined in.

"Does anyone else want to add to what they said?" Robin asked. "If not, we need to vote."

Everyone voted in favor of implementing the foster home into our program. We knew we would have to sit down and lay out a blueprint to get a general idea of exactly how we want to run the foster home and make it coincide with our project, but Robin assured us that it wouldn't be a problem. When our meeting was over I wrapped things up and headed home.

To my surprise, when I got home the house was quiet. The girls were sleep and Mike was alone in the living room looking like something was bothering him. The last time I saw that look on his face was when the doctors told him he couldn't play football again.

"Baby what's wrong?" I asked, as I sat down beside him.

"Lori's son got killed today."

"What! How?"

"A drive-by shooting; he was at the park playing basketball and got hit in the head. They caught the people responsible. Would you believe that three of the four guys were under age? How could an eleven, fourteen and sixteen year old be murderers? They're just throwing their lives away because they don't have any guidance. When I was growing up we had little league baseball, different age basketball leagues, afterschool programs, free breakfast and lunch programs."

"What's wrong with having all those things for the kids growing up now?"

"Nothing, it's jus-."

"It just sounds like you're about to make an excuse. You have to step up and make a difference. You have all the resources to make it happen."

"I guess you're right."

"You know I'm right."

We went over a few scenarios on how he could start his own non-profit organization that could bring back the things he spoke about, and then I went upstairs to get a much needed bath. As I was soaking in my hot soothing bubble bath, I kept asking myself if Mike's plan could've saved my brothers. I missed them so much and I have never stopped blaming myself for the trouble they constantly got themselves into and eventually got them killed. Maybe if I would've just spent more time with them. There had to be something I could've done. When I finally finished beating myself up mentally, I got dressed and said a prayer before I went to bed.

"Dear God, can you please find it in your many blessings that I seek to help me get through this mental torture I'm battling with. It's hard for me to find peace within myself, but if you can give me some type of assurance that my brothers are in your care it would make life so much easier for me. Dear God, I also ask that you give Mike a sense of direction, patience and willpower to reach out to and save those in need of his help. Thank you for listening. In Jesus name I pray AMEN!"

The next morning I woke up energized and instead of the normal two miles I ran every Monday through Friday, I ran four. It even carried over to when I went to the office. My energy traveled throughout the office and we all had a productive day. We had everything laid out on how we were going to implement the foster homes with the Boy's and Girl's clubs, plus after sharing Mike's vision with the City Councilman who was delighted that we accepted his offer, he had the backing he needed too. I don't know if my great day had anything to do with my prayer, but I took it as God's answer that my brothers were in good hands.

The first building done was the one we had in Homewood, so the Mayor arranged for a huge grand opening. Our whole staff participated in cutting the tape, and then we enjoyed the refreshments that awaited us inside. Jessica took the honors of taking our guest on their second tour, which they were impressed by. The first room she took them to was the study hall, where homework and reading was done. All the kids had to do an hour of the study hall before they even thought about entering any of the other rooms. If their homework wasn't done, the study hall would be the room of choice until it got done. No music, food or drinks were permitted in the study hall. As they continued down the hall, Jessica stopped at the Arts & Crafts room. This was where the kids could draw, paint, do pottery or any other concept they could come up with. The other rooms that she took them to were the music room, computer room, game room and the rubber room, where the cheerleaders would practice at. Every other location was designed the same way, so it could be easy to operate.

"We're very impressed with what we saw. I never had any doubts, but what you ladies have put together has gone well beyond my imagination," the Mayor told us when the tour was over.

"The most important thing is to put children in a comfort zone, to allow them to feel free and safe. The Boy's and Girl's clubs that you've designed gives them that," The City Councilman added.

"We're glad that everyone approves of what we've put together," Jessica shared.

"All of this was the easy part though. The true challenge comes in getting kids off the streets and helping them prosper. We have the patience and the determination, but they have to want it."

"I agree and they will want it," the Mayor added. "In the past there weren't many avenues for them, but thanks to you ladies they have opportunities to learn and be creative in so many different aspects. It may not happen overnight Jessica, but the BBNB Inc. will have a major impact on our community."

"I hope you're right because we have a lot of time and energy invested in our projects."

"Look outside the box for a second. If I were taking you on a tour of this place what would you think?" The Mayor asked.

"I would probably tell you that you have a lovely place here and that it's a beautiful environment for kids to feel comfortable."

"Is there anything else that needs to be said?"

"I guess not. We just don't want this to be a disappointment for us or the people supporting us."

"You can never be a disappointment. All of you have already made an impact by overcoming all the obstacles you faced in the past. All of you women are living examples that anything is possible if you fight for what you believe in."

The following week we had all the furniture and equipment installed at our Homewood location, which we paid for dearly. I forgot to call and have the alarm system put in and when we came back after the long weekend, all the computers were gone, the art supplies were gone, the furniture was cut up and the music room was destroyed. As I took all of that in, I felt violated like when I was raped. I wanted to go ball up in a corner but something inside of me told me to stand up and fight back. I threw aside the self-pity and got on top of my game. The first thing I did was called the insurance company, who told me that we had to wait two weeks before our property got replaced. In the meantime, I had the alarm system put in. Me and the girls hung around late and repainted or did whatever else was needed.

"Did you hear that noise?" Kelly asked me.

"Yeah, it sounded like it came from over by the window."

I walked outside to see what was going on and spotted a young guy with dark clothes on trying to pry open the window;

"What do you think you're doing?" I shouted, as I began walking towards him.

He pulled out a knife and started swinging it at me, but he was trying to find a way out rather than actually cut me. I studied his movement, then found the perfect opportunity to restrain him. With bricks in his pockets he couldn't have weighed a hundred and thirty pounds. As I was wrestling the knife off him, Kelly and the rest of the girls came running out.

"Get off me you crazy bitch!"

"I got your crazy bitch! Somebody call the police while I hold him down!"

"No please don't, I'll tell you where all your stuff is!"

"Where is it?" I shouted.

"Promise me no police! Nobody can know I told you either or they'll kill me!"

At the sounds of those words I picked him up off the ground and took him in the building. I could see the fear in his eyes, so I made sure my tone was low when I spoke.

"What's your name?" I asked.

He didn't respond. Instead he just scanned the room as if he was looking for an escape. Melissa walked up and stood beside me.

"We're not going to do anything to hurt you, nor will we call the police," Melissa explained. "If there's any type of way we can help you we will, but if you won't talk to us we'll have to call the police."

"My name is Roy."

"Roy what?" I asked.

"Roy Walton."

"Where do you live Roy?"

"It depends. Sometimes I stay over my friend's house or over different girl's house."

"How old are you? Where are your parents?" I continued to dig.

"I'm seventeen. My dad is dead and my mom is on crack."

"I'm sorry to hear that Roy. We can provide you with a place to stay if you want."

"I can't, they'll come find me."

"Who?"

"The gang I'm in or the one's we feud with. They told me the only way out was death."

"We can protect you. Let us help."

"I can't," he said, revealing a small black hand gun." I don't want to kill any of y'all, but I will."

We all backed away as he headed towards the door, watching his back every step of the way.

"You can find your stuff at 14 James Avenue. If you wait too long it won't be there," he told us before disappearing.

We immediately called the police and gave them the address Roy gave us, then I called Mike. They came over as fast as they could. As we told them everything that happened, I could see the rage forming in Mike's facial expression.

"These neighborhoods are too dangerous! Y'all might have to reconsider being in certain areas! It's not a safe environment for the children!"

"This is exactly where we need to be!" Kelly told him. "It's the children that are making it unsafe and we need to find a way to pull them off the streets! The guy tonight wanted help, but he was afraid!"

"If he wanted help why did he pull out a gun?"

"To make an escape!" I joined in. " I wrestled him down, then brought him inside. If he wanted to harm us, why would he tell us his name or where all our stuff that got stolen is?"

"How do you even know he gave you his real name?"

"I don't know if that's his real name, but I could see it in his eyes that he wanted to reach out for help, and he even said as much. He could've pulled the gun out when I first attacked him. I believe he thought I was going to back away when he pulled out the knife."

"You should have."

"I couldn't."

"We'll get into that when we get home. If the security doesn't get beefed up this project is over."

"Mike you knew this was a rough area when we got involved."

"And this is my way of responding to what happened today. I respect everything that you're doing, but I can't just sit back and allow y'all to be in harm's way."

We continued to go back and forth until I decided to give in. He was right, but we knew there were a lot of kids out there like Roy that needed our help and we couldn't turn our backs on them. To try to prevent a situation like that from happening again we talked to the Mayor about some extra security.

I don't know if Roy was really the young boy's name, but the tip he gave us about our belongings was accurate. We got everything but the art supplies back. Five juveniles were also arrested in the process. When we went to the police station to claim our property, we looked at photos of the juveniles and none of them was Roy, which meant he was still out there alone and afraid. I kept asking myself where he would go or if he would come back for our help. If and when he did return, he'd be well taken care of.

The Mayor held up his end and provided us with the security we needed for all our locations and we opened up to the public. Parents of the kids that joined stopped by to check things out and they all gave us their approval. They felt comfortable that their children would get the proper tutoring to help them with their education. In a lot of the Public Schools the teachers taught about Christopher Columbus and other stuff that wouldn't be relevant to everyday life as they grew up. Our goals were to simply help them comprehend what they read, give them a good understanding of mathematics and to teach them the morals and principles of giving respect in order to get it. In the beginning a lot of them were rough around the edges, but being stuck in the study hall took its toll and they eventually gave in.

The rest of our locations opened up, but we didn't have many members. We immediately took action though. Janet had a thousand fliers printed up and we went door to door in the neighborhoods of our locations and passed them out. Kelly even invited the parents by to see what we had to offer. The Mayor pulled more strings and had an advertisement played on the local radio station. That helped a great deal. Parents began to stop by with their children, and after seeing what we had to offer, they joined.

The location in Manchester was the one that required the most attention. Most of the young guys that signed up were drug dealers who saw the Boy's and Girl's clubs as a pickup spot for girls they wanted. They swore they were pretty boys, constantly flashing their money and bragging about the latest fashion they wore. The only reason why we didn't kick them out was because the young ladies didn't give them the time of day, and the more time they spent there, the less time they were on the streets. I was so pleased at how focused the young ladies were on their school work and learning how to be creative in a positive way. As time went on, those boys quit on their own. All they did was invest more time on those dangerous streets corners, which frightened me because I saw firsthand how the streets took people and swallowed them whole. They took my mother, my brothers and they continued to have my biological father in a choke hold. When I finally decided to go talk to them and convince them to come back, I learned that the City Task Force did a sweep and took all of them to jail for various drug crimes. It's a shame how they threw their lives away for instant gratification, and it wasn't until it was too late that they realized it. Some of those street thugs didn't have a caring bone in their body and they used the money they had as a tool to use and manipulate people, meanwhile their family were at home struggling to pay bills and put food on the table. Then when all comes to an end, they call to those same people that were disregarded for love, support and money. Those were the ones that needed to be confined in a jail cell to learn morals and principles about respect and integrity.

Mike changed the concept of what we came up with for him and started a cleaning company for the youths. Their jobs were to clean the sidewalks in the morning and evenings on weekends and in the evening on weekdays. He found twelve people that were willing to coach baseball and started a Little League and Pony League. Also during the summer, he started a basketball league for fourteen and under, eighteen and under, along with an adult league. The location for the games was at Manchester field, held on Saturday's and Sunday's. Violence and drug dealing didn't come to a complete halt, but Mike's projects were a huge success and they created opportunities for everyone to do something constructive.

Our projects were a success as well and the opening of the foster home helped place children in a loving environment and as promised, the City Councilman helped us open up more throughout the city. We also opened up a few homeless shelters for the adults that didn't have a place to go or who couldn't afford a meal. It was depressing for me to see people in downtown Pittsburgh sitting in front of department stores in the middle of the winter with a dirty blanket filled with holes in it, holding a cup out asking for change. I couldn't walk around and act like none of that existed, so I went into action and we opened up four homeless shelters, where I personally did volunteer work once a week at each of them. I even took my daughters along to give them some understanding of the importance to give back.

As the summer began to wind down, I came across an article in the paper that brought tears to my eyes. I had to read it five times to make sure I wasn't making a mistake or seeing things. It read:

A seventeen year old was found dead on Race Street in Homewood. He died from multiple shots to the head. Witnesses have identified the victim as Roy Walton of Monticello Street. There are no suspects or leads in the case. If anyone has any tips that could help the investigation, please contact Commander Johnathon Stone at #555-1212.

As I continued to glance at the newspaper, I was overwhelmed with guilt for not being able to save Roy. I had difficulty sleeping, but when we went to the small funeral to pay our respects, I felt a sense of closure. We made sure he had a nice burial and I asked God if he could please embrace Roy as he did my brothers.

The music rooms were barely occupied at the Boy's and Girl's clubs, so we decided to turn it into a performing arts class equipped with a state of the art recording studio. We didn't actually know where we were going with this, it was just an attempt to make use of our music rooms. A talent was discovered that was right up under me and I never knew it existed. When my daughter Karen sung Mariah Carey's "Vision of Love," I almost broke down in tears.

"Come here baby. Where did you learn to sing like that?"

"In the bathroom. I always sing when I'm in the bathtub or shower."

"You never sung for me."

"I'm sorry."

"You don't have to be sorry."

"Mommy! I can rap like Lil' Kim!" Bria shouted, full of excitement.

"No baby. We rather you dance like Janet Jackson or Aaliyah," Kelly told her, as we all chuckled.

Karen's courage to sing in front of everyone opened up doors for others to step up and showcase their talent. Believe me when I tell you, there were a whole lot of kids with talent. As they got more comfortable performing in front of people, we sponsored local talent shows so the rest of the community could be a witness. They got great responses too.

The BBNB Inc. had taken great strides, but we couldn't save everyone. The good news was that well over three thousand people including the Boy's and Girl's clubs, foster homes and homeless shelters experienced firsthand how devoted we were to helping our precious community. We were pleased, but not satisfied with that amount and we continued to reach out to those in need, even those that didn't want it.

I didn't stop there. I was still actively involved in the fight against Domestic Violence and Sexual Abuse. I went to local meetings once a week and was asked to join a three month tour around the world to share my testimony which after discussing it with my husband and the sisterhood, I graciously accepted. I felt obligated to let the women, young ladies and young boys of the world know that we shouldn't and cannot allow the sickness of others to defeat us and stop us from doing what we wanted to do in life.

During my trip to Minnesota, I was encouraged to fight for the people even harder. When I heard some of the stories about young boys being molested by their fathers and other relatives, me and Jessica came to mind. She stayed silent and her situation almost destroyed her. After sharing my story, I encouraged people to be more vocal and not be afraid to reach out for help.

The issue of young boys being molested was starting to spread like wildfires. A lot of athletes confided in coaches or trainers and became victims of the sexual predators that roam the locker rooms seeking an opportunity. Most people who were victims didn't come out and speak about it until they became adults. Some just decided to live with those demons. By remaining silent, there's a great chance that someone else would become a victim of that monster. I confided in Robin and look where I am today. I will continue to fight for the physical, mental and emotional freedom that we're entitled to, but we can't be afraid to fight back. **THAT'S THE ONLY WAY WE'LL WIN.**

EPILOGUE...

That following summer was a busy one for all of us. Jessica and her boyfriend of three years found out they were having a baby and immediately got married. It was a beautiful ceremony and to see Jessica glowing and looking so happy made me think about the great strides she had taken to get where she was. She was so comfortable within herself that she found it in her heart to forgive her uncle. He didn't personally know how she felt, but through prayer she asked God to forgive him for his sins and to cure him of his sickness.

Mont and Robin were closer than ever, but they both constantly told us that they didn't need someone's signature to prove that they belonged to each other. For a person that didn't personally know their situation, they would swear Mont and Robin were happily married.

Kelly eventually decided to tie the knot. She was content with how things were, but her parents had a hand in on mentally twisting her wrist to walk down the aisle. She ended up doing so and it was one of the happiest times of our lives. Kelly by far, was the most beautiful bride I ever seen.

Janet wasn't with being attached at all. Ty was the only man she dealt with even though they had an open relationship. All she wanted was three nights a week and he was free to do what he wanted. The average man would've taken that opportunity to explore every option he could, but the other four days a week he devoted to their non-profit organizations.

Although she was a long way from getting married, Melissa was in a serious relationship with one of the star players for the Pittsburgh Pirates. He treated her like the queen that she is and he earned our love and respect.

The Sisterhood continued to be a strong unit and our brand continued to soar to new heights. We began to expand our franchise to different cities, who embraced us with no hesitation.

The thing that affected us all was the death of Momma Sue. She died at the young age of fifty-one from breast cancer. Momma Sue was a strong and courageous woman that taught us core values of how to conduct and apply ourselves. She installed the proper morals and principles in us to help us become the women we are today. Although a large part of our hearts had dissolved, we replenished them when we started the Momma Sue foundation for breast cancer awareness. Mr. Damon died two years later from depression. When he lost her, he no longer had a will to live.

Besides from constantly being active in the communities, my immediate family lived a normal, but pleasant life. It was amazing to see the development of my two daughters and how Karen grew as a singer.

She had a bright side and great future coming, but her father told her that high school had to be finished first. As for Bria, she continued to be mommy's little girl.

As a whole I wish that a lot of things could've been different, but the experiences we go through define our character. So even though there's a point in time that we have to learn to live with regrets, it's important to embrace what we've been through and to keep striving to be better. My name is Keya Gibson-Carson and I thank you for coming along on my life's journey with me.

THE END!

COMING SOON...

CAN'T BE LOVE

AFTER THOUGHT...

    The motivation behind me writing this book was to push the envelope on my creativity and to share my visions from a woman's perspective. Furthermore, it's also because of the guilt I feel of me pursing street dreams and leaving all the women in my life vulnerable to all the cruelty and danger that life has to offer. To all the women of the world, I hope and pray that this book represents your stance towards domestic violence and sexual abuse. A woman was not placed on this earth to be battered, bruised or beaten mentally, emotionally or physically. It took me a long time to learn and understand, but women are to be loved, cherished and respected at all times. You're here to willingly help with the reproduction of our society. A chain is only strong as its weakest link and together ladies, y'all can develop enough strength and courage to fight back and win all battles. With the overwhelming number of so many men being incarcerated, the world has become dominated by women. Learn your true self-worth ladies and don't be comfortable with being labeled as a bitch or hoe. I take full responsibility for the women that I manipulated and lied to and who now have low self-esteem issues, but please don't allow my ignorance to deter you from recognizing your inner and outer beauty regardless if you're dark, light, short, tall skinny or big. All of you are beautiful in your own way. Some of you are just so desperate for love and affection that you go against your morals and principles just to receive instant gratification. In order to totally understand life and get a true grasp on it you have to learn to love yourself first and foremost. When you get a grasp on loving yourself, you'll see firsthand that **Love's Not Supposed To Hurt** and you'll see to it that it doesn't. Stand up ladies! The little girls looking for guidance need you. The men worthy of love need you. Most importantly, the world needs you. God laid out a blueprint for all to follow. Try it and watch all the wonderful experiences you encounter during your journey.

GOD BLESS YOU MY QUEENS...

I'm from the north side of Pittsburgh, PA. Right now I am currently finishing up a 188 month federal sentence for drug conspiracy that began in 2002. I always had a passion for writing, so during many sleepless nights I taught myself how to write novels. Upon my release in 2016, I plan on starting a variety of non-profit organizations. I want to give young men a fighting chance, so they won't have to experience the life I have. I also want to bring awareness to the young women out there, with hopes of them living an abuse free life.

A SMALL PIECE OF ADVICE...

If anyone reading this book is going through some type of Domestic Violence or Sexual Abuse or have gone through a situation, please seek counseling and get some type of understanding on how to fight those demons that have occupied space inside of you. Don't become immune to abuse, because it's not normal. Mental and emotional abuse is not healthy either. Once again, I encourage you to act now, because all the true luxuries of life await you.

OTHER BOOKS COMING SOON...

All Money, Ain't Good Money- (Tommy Shorter)

All Money, Ain't Good Money II- (Tommy Shorter)

All Money, Ain't Good Money III - (Tommy Shorter)

Can't Be Love - (Tommy Shorter)

Misled - (Tommy Shorter)

It's Hip To Be Square - (Tommy Shorter)

Da Game Don't Love Me - (Tommy Shorter)

Misconception of Love - (Tommy Shorter)

Hard Time - (Tommy Shorter)

You, Me & He - (Tommy Shorter)

ALSO COMING SOON…

Cracked Out - (Raymond Sweetenburg)

Vulnerable Man - (Raymond Sweetenburg)

Var - (Raymond Sweetenburg)

LOVE'S NOT SUPPOSED TO HURT

CRACKED OUT

It's a cool 82° degrees in Riviera Beach. The smell of salt was emitting from the Atlantic Ocean several miles away. As the sun slowly descended, the eyes of the hopeful appeared, awaiting their disguise. I quickly shot out of my hiding place as small droplets of rain began to fall, giving moister to my dry, pale skin. With the fear that someone or something was watching me, waiting to attack. I headed up into the path that lead through the 30th Street grave yard. There were no visible signs or fence describing the name or who resides there, so we gave it the name for our own purposes. It described to us the dead and the living dead that moved about whether in spirit or human form. It carried the look of a sand pit with weeds and stones sticking out of the ground. If I was to walk you through you wouldn't have an idea that we were standing in a grave yard, unless I tell you. The farther I walked into the darkness that started to consume the area small trickles of tears began to escape my eyes. Hearing a noise, I looked around for the presence of someone, only to see my shadow from the reflection of light shining from the light pole ahead. I grabbed at my heart that was beating at a rate abnormal for my small frame. Staring as guilt, remorse, regret and loneliness played with my emotions as the high that I received only moments earlier slowly dissipated. They say gravesites were sacred ground, a place where the dead rest. But how could that be when I'm disturbed and they say I looked like the walking dead. When I have witnessed rape, extortion, murder and the tears of the broken hearted, not for the dead, but for the pain of another hit of drugs whether it be pipe, can or needle here.

"I have to stop using," I cried out to God, my mother and the life that has been placed before me. "Why Lord. Momma help me. Is this the life I'm supposed to live? I want to be a regular kid." I continued, taking slow steps through the sand, thinking about my struggles of tomorrow. My pain of today and the childhood that I would never have.

Here I am 10½ years old, sprung out on crack cocaine. Can you imagine the most memorable moment in your life was the day that you smoked free base? The day that your life changed forever. The day that you learned to overcome obstacles stacked against you from a generational curse. The day that all your dreams were lost. Your friends became your enemies. Your family became the prey. And you became your worst nightmare. Who was to blame, God, man, self, religion, family, friends, the system, love, hatred or a curse placed by the fingers of God. Walk with me on a journey of one of the most prolific stories ever told.

Raymond Sweetenburg

Connect with Tommy Shorter on Social Media and www.tommyshorter.com.

Facebook.com/thetommyshorter

Instagram.com/tommyshorter

Made in the USA
Columbia, SC
17 July 2020